SHANGÓ

JAMES ROBERTO CURTIS

For Dan Gade,
Geographer, traveler, a
scholar in the classic Tradition,
and one of my major heroes,

Arte Público Press
Houston, Texas
1996

James Roberto Curtis
2003

This volume is made possible through grants from the National Endowment for the Arts (a federal agency) and the Andrew W. Mellon Foundation.

Recovering the past, creating the future

Arte Público Press
University of Houston
Houston, Texas 77204-2090

Cover illustration and design by Gladys Ramirez

Curtis, James R., 1947–
    Shangó / by James Roberto Curtis.
        p.   cm.
    ISBN 1-55885-096-1 (pbk. : alk. paper)
    1. Cuban Americans—Florida—Miami—Fiction. 2. Anthropologists—Florida—Miami—Fiction. 3. Police—Florida—Miami—Fiction. 4. Miami (Fla.)—Fiction. 5. Santería—Fiction. I. Title.
PS3553.U713S53   1996
813'.54—dc20   95-37664
                                                    CIP

The paper used in this publication meets the requirements of the American National Standard for Permanence of Paper for Printed Library Materials Z39.48-1984. ∞

For Patti.

See, I told you I could do it!

SHANGÓ

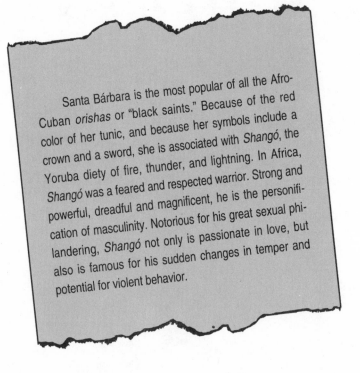

Santa Bárbara is the most popular of all the Afro-Cuban *orishas* or "black saints." Because of the red color of her tunic, and because her symbols include a crown and a sword, she is associated with *Shangó*, the Yoruba diety of fire, thunder, and lightning. In Africa, *Shangó* was a feared and respected warrior. Strong and powerful, dreadful and magnificent, he is the personification of masculinity. Notorious for his great sexual philandering, *Shangó* not only is passionate in love, but also is famous for his sudden changes in temper and potential for violent behavior.

K. Christopher Ward, *Catholic Saints and African Gods* (Austin: University of Texas Press, 1989).

1
AN IMMANENCE OF EVIL

Even by sultry Miami standards it was oppressively hot and muggy for 4:23 in the morning. At least, that's what Lieutenant Osvaldo Gutiérrez thought as he flipped the fan on the Ford's a/c to high speed and accelerated onto I-95 westbound, headed for the Dolphin Expressway. The .38-caliber Smith & Wesson service revolver, in a plainclothes holster shafted on his left side, felt as heavy as the damage it could inflict. But the heaviness was in itself reassuring. The lieutenant's stomach gurgled. Although he'd slugged down cups of *café cubano* throughout the evening, he'd skipped dinner. Images of the murder scene six years ago and the photos in the case file of the other up in Jersey had forewarned him: The less he had in his stomach the better. Let it growl, he thought.

The Ford exited at the NW 17th Avenue ramp, sped north across the Miami River, hung a sharp left on North River Drive and coasted the half mile to where the squad car waited, its flashing red light a pulsating beacon through the heavy night air.

"Lieutenant Gutiérrez?"

He nodded.

"I'm Patrolman Ruiz, Orlando Ruiz. At roll call Sergeant Ward's orders were to radio Communications immediately if we suspected..."

"Right," Gutiérrez interrupted. "Then you were in the area when the call went out?"

"No, sir. I mean there wasn't a call. We were on patrol, Officer Cruz and I, when the old man over there flagged us down."

He nodded toward the squad car, where two heads were visible through the rear window.

"He's a wino, an old river rat. Said he was looking for a place to sleep. Couldn't get much more out of him, though. No ID, no fixed address. He's pretty incoherent. Shitfaced, I guess."

"Where's the body, Ruiz?"

"Over there, sir...the wooden building...small one next to the river, with the tin roof. I went inside but,..." he trailed off. "I've never imagined anything like...like that. Good thing he was drunk—the wino I mean."

The patrolman's face was pasty white and glistened with sweat; he had a faintly sour smell about him. He couldn't have been more than 22, Gutiérrez estimated.

"I'd like to question him after I've looked around a bit, so keep him in the squad car until I get back. And send the Crime Scene people on down when they arrive. They should be here shortly."

Gutiérrez straightened the jacket of his tailored suit and turned to go, then turned back, somewhat pensively, to face the young cop. "You know, Ruiz, after all these years the sight of violent death, of murdered victims lying there in their own blood, still curdles my insides." He shrugged his shoulders. "Guess I'll never get used to it, if I haven't by now."

Ruiz watched Gutiérrez straighten his jacket once again and then stride into the darkness toward the river. So this was Lieutenant Gutiérrez, his tailored suits a trademark around the Department. But never flamboyant; never like some of the younger studs with their bigger-than-life-full-of-bullshit-bravado and exaggerated self-confidence. Not that Gutiérrez was like many of the older ones—overly cautious, even paranoid, just trying to survive until they could retire. No, Gutiérrez was a different sort. Quiet, something that was rare among cops these days. Somewhat of a loner, at least in recent years. But not aloof or full of himself. Osvaldo Gutiérrez was a class act, was the general consensus, and after this first meeting, Ruiz had no reason to doubt it.

The building, more accurately a shed, was at the back edge of a vacant lot, overgrown with weeds and littered with rotting boats, oil drums and discarded crab traps, and about 50 or 60 feet from the street. Gutiérrez stopped a few feet away, lit a cigar, and forcibly exhaled the acrid smoke. Experience had taught him it was best to mask the stench of death. Cigars usually did the trick. He hoped it would this time.

An ethereal reddish glow escaped through the half-opened door. He paused before going in. The lieutenant had sensed before this unmistakable immanence of evil. Involuntarily his right hand moved to the handle of the .38, then fell back. The door swung open easily, and a rush of warm, fetid air greeted him. A headless black rooster lay crumpled on the threshold. Gutiérrez stepped over the mass of matted feathers and walked in.

From the ceiling hung a single low-wattage red bulb. The flickering of a candle flame sporadically intensified the soft reddish hue that bathed the room. On the walls and on a wooden workbench were boat motors, parts and assorted marine supplies. But Gutiérrez scarcely noticed them. His eyes were drawn instead to an altar in the middle of the floor.

Lying limp across a large black cauldron was a goat, its disemboweled remains forming a pool of dark and lumpy matter. The floor was slick with grease and blood. On top of the carcass was a human skull, crowned with three half-melted votive candles. Thin streams of caked blood coursed down beneath the candle wax into the eye sockets and around the gold-lined teeth.

Supine at the base of the altar was the body of a man, naked from the waist up, a garland of red carnations and white chrysanthemums around his neck, a double-bladed ax buried in his chest. A scab of flies swarmed about the gaping wound.

Gutiérrez turned, pulled a handkerchief from his back pocket and wiped his face. He felt nauseous. His eyes closed momentarily as his face moved away from the source of the stench. He puffed heavily on the cigar. But it didn't help.

When the lieutenant turned his face back around, he noticed that the handle of the ax was covered with alternating stripes of red and white tape. Closer now, he leaned over the body, his hands on his knees. The victim's eyes were bulging, gleaming like polished stones. He looked Latin, maybe 30, 35 years old, Gutiérrez decided. But unutterable horror, or perhaps ecstacy, was frozen on the dead face. Gutiérrez was not certain.

Standing now, the lieutenant looked more closely about the room. Three—no four—decapitated white chickens marinating in their own blood were scattered about, pieces of candy corn stuck to their blood-smeared feathers. Beside the altar a round, 12-hour candle burned. Next to the candle and cut open were two watermelons, a cantaloupe, several bananas strung together with red and white ribbon, and a small wooden box. Carefully stepping over to the box, Gutiérrez bent down and removed the top using his handkerchief so as to not leave fingerprints.

A plaster Santa Bárbara stared at him from the depths of the box.

"*Shangó*," Gutiérrez muttered out loud, shaking his head slowly from side to side.

In the distance the sound of approaching loud men's voices. "Watch that pile of barf!" one of them yelled.

The first through the door was Homicide Detective Leroy Dukes.

"Holy... Fucking... Shit!"

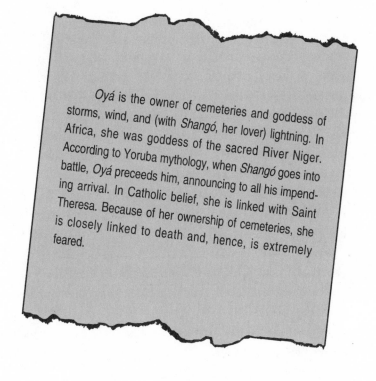

Oyá is the owner of cemeteries and goddess of storms, wind, and (with *Shangó*, her lover) lightning. In Africa, she was goddess of the sacred River Niger. According to Yoruba mythology, when *Shangó* goes into battle, *Oyá* preceeds him, announcing to all his impending arrival. In Catholic belief, she is linked with Saint Theresa. Because of her ownership of cemeteries, she is closely linked to death and, hence, is extremely feared.

Robert Peterson, *Alternative Belief Systems* (Oakland: The People's Daily Report, 1993).

2

AIN'T BILLY DREAMIN'?

Two Weeks Earlier

Billy wiped a circle on the foggy window. Thunder at night always scared him, made him get up and peek out across the street toward the graveyard. In disbelief he rubbed his sleepy eyes, then rubbed them again. But there they were. A ghost. And a giant. And a dwarf, a little colored dwarf. Marcus say that place was a haunted. Yeah, he say ghosts and bogeymen do their business over there.

Billy's eyes shot to the mantel clock. Two-fifteen a.m. Whew! Safe! Marcus tol' him bogeymen only come out at midnight. "That's when you gotta look out, boy!" That what he always say. And Marcus smart 'bout such things. Whew! But, maybe that ghost and them never learnt to tell time when they was in school. Else...they just like to misbehave. He better see what they doin'.

Trembling knees on the couch, one eye covered, Billy's head rose slowly to the circle on the window.

They were at the corner beneath the street light. The colored dwarf had a dove in one hand, a rooster in the other. A big black rooster. He give the dove to the ghost. And it disappear. Poof. Gone. The giant grab that black rooster 'round the neck. He lift him way, way over his head. The rooster don't like it way up there. He really squawk and beat his wings. The giant say something out loud to the corner! Then he pet the rooster. And throw him in the street. The rooster jerk 'round and 'round like he ain't got no head. Uh, oh...

Billy sunk back into the couch. They misbehavin' all right! He better get Marcus, let him see. He never gonna believe this. Aaah, man. Marcus at the Pinder's tonight.

Billy pulled the covers up around him. Mama don't 'preciate it when somebody wake her up, 'less they sick. He tell her in the mornin'. You watch. She gonna say, "Baby, you dreamin', that's all. Ain't no ghosts over there." Mama sweet. But she don't know 'bout no bogeymen.

Billy inched back toward the window. What they up to now?

They steppin' backwards into the graveyard! Now they walkin' 'round real slow. Like they was countin' them ol' tombs. The ones up on the ground. For dead people that don't like all that dirt 'round 'em. That what Granny say before she pass away. "Don't y'all stick me in no hole in the ground. When Gabriel's horn blow on Judgement Day, I wanna hear it!"

Hey, they over by Granny's! Standin' 'round. Boy, she be mad! Granny don't tolerate no misbehavin'. Mama say Granny a do-right woman.

Uh, oh... What that dwarf got? That a knife? A big ol' machete? He tryin' to...cut open that tomb? Don't he know, you do that spooks come flyin' out. Bad spooks!

Yep. That what they doin'. Look at the giant. He pushin' the top off! Oooh, oh. There go the spooks!

Billy yanked the covers over his head. Spooks get mad if you see 'em. Real mad, boy. He felt dizzy. And his tummy ached. Like when he got sick on the loop-d-loop at the fair. But if he hide now, Marcus gonna call him a scaredy-cat. A sissy. He gonna wanna know what they do next. Maybe them spooks done gone.

Only his eyes peering from the covers, Billy pressed his nose against the window. Whew! They goin'. The giant gettin' in a car. He gonna drive. The dwarf carryin' a sack. Here come the ghost. What's it got in its hand? Something...white and...round. Uh, oh...

Billy heard noise out in the street. He woke with a start,
then sprung off the couch. He glanced at the clock: 7:14. He
pulled on his pants and threw open the front door. Police cars
were parked in front of his house. In the graveyard, cops and
men in suits were walking around looking at the ground, taking pictures. He better get over there fast, tell 'em what he
saw.

The grass was wet. Billy didn't like to walk barefooted in
the graveyard. It gave him the willys. But he didn't have time
to put on his shoes.

A black policeman waved for Billy to stop, then ambled
over. "Sorry, sonny," he said, "you can't come in here right
now."

"There's a tomb open, ain't there," Billy said.

The cop eyed him closely. "What makes you think that?"

"'Cause I seen 'em do it."

The policeman raised his eyebrows. "You sure about
that?"

Billy nodded. "Sure, I'm sure."

"Okay, then," the cop said. "Why don't you tell me who
you saw?"

"A ghost. And a giant. And a dwarf."

The man paused, then laughed heartily and patted Billy
on the head.

Billy stamped his foot. "I did, mister. You gotta believe
me."

The cop looked at Billy's wet feet and then up at his big
pleading eyes. "Sure I believe you, sonny." He pulled a pad of
paper from his back pocket. "I'll see it gets in the report. Now
you better get on back home, 'fore you step in something you
don't wanna step in." He smiled.

Billy glanced around the policeman toward the tomb,
where a bunch of people were milling around. That was the

one all right. His shoulders slumped. He felt a lump in his throat. "Oh, no..." he whimpered out loud, tears starting to roll from his eyes. "Not that one!"

Head Stolen from Coffin
Santería Cultists Suspected

A coffin in the Charlotte Jane Memorial Cemetery in Coconut Grove was broken into Friday night and a woman's head removed, investigators said Saturday.

"It is the second such case in Dade County in the last decade," said Lieutenant Osvaldo Gutiérrez.

"We suspect followers of santería were responsible for this," Gutiérrez said. "They must have wanted the head to use in one of their rituals."

The tomb that was robbed held the remains of Elizabeth Mary Rolle. Born in Nassau in 1911, Mrs. Rolle had lived in the Grove since 1934. She died of heart failure in 1990. Mrs. Rolle was the mother of four and grandmother of seven.

"This is a nightmare for us," said Queenesther Brown, Rolle's daughter. "Why my mother? Why her? She never hurt nobody, not a soul."

Rolle worked in housekeeping at Mercy Hospital for 15 years. She was a founding member of the New Day Baptist Church.

A dead rooster and a pigeon, both decapitated, were found at the scene. Investigators also found a long machete-type knife, covered with black and green stripes of tape.

Dr. Henry Krajewski, a professor of anthropology at the University of Miami and an expert on the santería cult, explained that this was most unusual. "Santería is not normally involved with acts of this kind. It typically is used for good or protective purposes. But little is known of its practice in the U.S.," he said.

The voodoo-like cult was born in Cuba from a mixture of Catholicism and African tribal religions.

Apparently the rooster and pigeon were sacrificed to appease specific gods.

"Eleggua, the god of roads, gates and doors who controls communication with the other deities," Krajewski said, "requires the blood of a black rooster. Pigeons are sacrificed to Oya, considered the goddess of cemeteries."

Krajewski explained that the black and green tape on the machete is associated with the god Ogun, the owner of iron and weapons who is often invoked in malevolent acts.

The thieves might have chosen Rolle's coffin because of its location: seventh in line from the corner of the cemetery and in from the street, Dr. Krajewski ventured.

"In santería, seven is a very powerful number, symbolic of the seven African warrior gods," he said.

Professor Krajewski refused to speculate on why the head was stolen. But Lieutenant Gutiérrez stated, "I'd be surprised if we don't come across it again."

Six years ago a skull was stolen from a local cemetery under similar circumstances. Later, it was found at the scene of a ritualistic murder. The victim, a convicted drug dealer, was believed to have been involved in santería.

Gutiérrez, who investigated the case, said, "I hope this doesn't mean what I think it means."

In Florida, desecrating a grave or disturbing its contents is a first-degree misdemeanor punishable by a maximum one-year jail term and a $1,000 fine.

"Our family don't care about all that voodoo talk," said Mrs. Brown. "We just can't understand how this could happen. Why can't the dead be left alone?"

3
TOO COOL

Miguel Calderón squeezed two thin lines of suntan lotion down the back of Vicki's legs and smiled wolfishly as his hand glided over her warm, smooth skin. The milky-white lotion called TROPICAL SUN—"For that dark, natural tan of the islands"—smelled of coconuts. He liked it. It was the smell of paradise, he thought.

Sitting back on his haunches, Miguel shaded his eyes as he gazed across the beach toward the turquoise waters of the Atlantic, bright and dazzling on a clear sunny day. Farther out, in the Gulf Stream, where the sea turned a deep, inky blue, a large oil tanker pushed slowly south, bucking the powerful current. A couple of hundred miles in that direction lay Cuba, where he was born 23 years before in the small beach town of Santa Fe, just west of Havana. Memories of Cuba didn't make him particularly nostalgic though. He hadn't lived on the island in 18 years, and his childhood there was now just a vague, curious memory. In fact, at times he felt he'd never really lived there at all. Life was so different here, in Miami, only 200 miles away, but it might as well have been the other side of the planet.

Miguel's eyes shifted from the tanker to the beach, all powdery white and shimmering on this Sunday in early fall. Along the shore he spotted an elderly couple—Jewish, he figured—who were carrying their shoes. Otherwise they were fully dressed. Looking around, he noticed that other people were staring at them as well. It was odd, he mused, how beaches were the only public places where the more clothes you had on the more suspect you became.

Vicki definitely wasn't suspect.

The greasy brown bottle of TROPICAL SUN squirted out a blob of the coconut-scented lotion. Across the back of her long legs his hand moved again, up and down. Finally it slipped inside her pink-and-green bikini, and he gently pinched her rump. She had a cute behind, shaped like an apple and, he marveled, nearly as hard.

She peered back at him over the red sunglasses perched on the end of her nose. "All right, Calderón, don't get carried away. At least not yet..."

"Hey?" he pleaded, patting her ass. "I was just checking to see if a butt this perfect is real."

She wrinkled her nose at him and laid her head back down, trying hard not to squint. Oh, how she loathed squint lines.

Miguel stared appreciatively at the golden body stretched languorously before him. Vicki was about five-eight, with medium-length blond hair, large green eyes and a well-scrubbed, athletic appearance. She was the picture of health and vitality, an All-American, sexy-sweet girl. Perhaps, as befit the cliché, she wasn't one of the brightest students on campus. But what the hell, Miguel reasoned, who wants a fucking rocket scientist for a girlfriend? Besides, she was a great lay.

"Too bad that lotion doesn't taste as good as it smells," he said, dabbing the tip of his tongue with a towel. "Guess what I'd spread it with if it did?"

"Oh, brother," Vicki moaned, rolling over onto her back. "Think I know who's horny today."

"Every day, woman, every day."

"Right, macho man. Sometimes I think you're more Cuban than you'd like everyone to believe. Much more Cuban."

"You thin' so, huh?" he said in a surprisingly good impersonation of Ricky Ricardo. Then he sang out, *Babaluuuu....*"

Vicki tried not to smile, a strategy in her battle against squint lines. But she loved it when Miguel did Ricky. "I Love Lucy" was her all-time favorite TV show.

"Didn't Desi Arnaz grow up here?" she asked.

"Graduated from Miami High."

"Really? Is that where you went to school?"

"No, I went to South Miami High. The Cobras."

"The Cobras?"

"That was our school mascot. Our favorite cheer went: 'Lean to the left, lean to the right, stand up, sit down, bite bite bite.'"

Having been a cheerleader herself, Vicki really appreciated the call and laughed out loud, momentarily suffering a setback in the war against squint lines.

Miguel stood and stretched. "Think I'll take a swim. Join me?" he asked, although he knew she'd say no. She once informed him that the ocean was so polluted and salt water like *totally destroyed* her hair.

She sat up and considered her glistening body. "Maybe later, okay? I still haven't read the paper."

He glanced over at the six-inch-thick Sunday edition of the *Herald*.

Vicki watched him as he jogged down to the shore, waded out a few feet and dove in. He emerged swimming in long, powerful strokes straight out to sea for nearly 50 yards where he stopped, looked back and waved.

Too cool were the only words she could think of to describe their last four months together. Since that first night when they'd met at a beach party, the one thrown by a group of anthropology graduate students to celebrate the end of the spring semester, they'd been seeing each other steadily. In spite of his macho posturing—which didn't really bother her; it was all show, she knew—Miguel was perfect. Handsome, tall (about six-one), thick black hair, big sensitive brown eyes, classical Latin features—like a bullfighter, she liked to think—and such a sweetie. He sent her flowers, gave her chocolates, the whole crazy nine yards.

She'd heard that Cuban guys were like that, but Miguel was the first she'd ever dated. Frankly, she was surprised to be taken by it all. Kind of corny. For she considered herself an independent woman, supporting herself for nearly two years teaching aerobics at a club down in Kendall and with occasional modeling. But for some reason she had to admit she liked the feeling of being protected, cared for. Yeah, too cool, she thought.

Miguel now stood knee-deep in the water tossing a brightly colored beach ball to a little girl who squealed something in Spanish. He was in great shape, not an ounce of fat. And physical fitness was important to her, always had been. Even more than Miguel's handsome face and good build, she loved the way they looked together—the tall dark Latin guy with the beautiful blond at his side. All her friends said they were a perfect couple. Maybe that's what pleased her most of all. She often wondered if they had children what they'd look like. Lucky to have such pretty parents.

When Miguel splashed out of the surf, Vicki was reading the paper. He picked up a towel and began drying off vigorously. "Any more beer left?"

She ignored the question, her eyes glued to the paper.

"What's so interesting?"

She raised her hand. "Let me finish this, okay?"

He took a can of Bud Light out of the cooler and slipped it into an aquamarine foam holder with MIAMI DOLPHINS across it in orange.

Off to his right, in the shade of a row of the Australian pines that separated the beach from the parking lot beyond, he saw a group of Haitians dancing limp-limbed around the biggest fucking ghetto blaster he'd ever seen. He listened to the music for a while, not understanding the Creole lyrics but enjoying what he finally decided was reggae with a touch of salsa. They seemed so gentle and naive, the Haitians, just glad to be here. It was interesting how much blacker they were than most American blacks, and so African in the loose way they moved. And the clothes they wore—those big fat mamas in their shifts with native prints and bright island colors and the guys in their polyester pants and plaid shirts and hard shoes without socks. You could always spot the Haitians.

Vicki looked up. "I can't *believe* this story. It's so sick," she said, dragging the words.

He frowned. "What happened?"

"Remember that old cemetery over in the black Grove. The one on Charles Avenue, down from the Taurus Restaurant, where you took me on our first date?"

"Sure, what about it?"

"Well, night before last somebody broke into a coffin and stole a woman's head. You know, a skull."

Miguel wrinkled his brow and said more to himself than to her, "What the hell would they want with a skull?"

"It says here they suspect it was that cult..." She glanced down at the paper. "*Santería.*"

He smiled at the way she pronounced the word, and repeated it out loud using the proper accent, putting emphasis on the "i".

"Abuela, my grandmother, says their rituals are pretty weird—animal sacrifice, trance possession, that sort of thing."

Vicki was clearly fascinated. "Really? Your grandmother knows something about it, *santería?*"

He nodded. "Back home in Cuba her family had a maid, an old black woman named Sara. She was a *santera*. Abuela was a young girl then, and Sara taught her a few things. But she doesn't talk that much about it. Just that she's seen things. That she respects it."

Vicki was so fascinated that she forgot all about avoiding those squint lines. "Wow!" she bubbled. "They're quoting an anthropology professor from the university. You don't know a Professor Krajewski, do you? He's supposed to be an expert on the cult."

Miguel's mouth dropped. "Professor Krajewski? Christ! He's my ethnology prof!"

Vicki's eyes got big. "Omigod, are you kidding? Here, you gotta read this."

He sat down on the cooler, took a long pull on the Bud Light and began to read.

Miguel tossed the paper next to Vicki and stood up. He gazed out to sea.

"Kind of creepy, huh?" Vicki said.

He didn't bother to answer.

Finally she asked, "What are you thinking about?"

He looked down at her, an expression on his face that she'd never seen before. "Think I'll stop by the professor's office tomorrow and have a little chat. I'd like to ask him about all this stuff."

Vicki crossed her legs, now sitting Indian style, and leaned toward Miguel, grinning mischievously. In a lower voice she said, "Don't you wonder what it looked like? You know, the woman. After all that time... It must've been totally *gross*. Ouuuuuu." She shivered.

Miguel admired her firm little boobs, the white below the tan line showing. "For what it's worth, I don't know why they had to *steal* a skull. Hell, they sell 'em in *botánicas*. You could just walk in and buy one, no big deal."

Vicki looked astonished. "Really? In a what?"

"A *botánica*. It's a store that sells the...things they use in *santería* ceremonies."

"Here in Miami?"

He laughed. "Of course. Must be 25 or 30 of 'em, mainly in Little Havana and over in Hialeah. There's one near my house. That's where I saw the skulls."

Vicki began to rock back and forth, her head tilted, smiling coyly at him, waiting.

He knew the look, knew she wanted him to take her there. Why not? he decided. It couldn't hurt.

"Hey," he said, as if the idea had just dawned on him, playing along, "maybe we could stop by there on the way to my place. Sound all right?"

Too cool, Vicki thought.

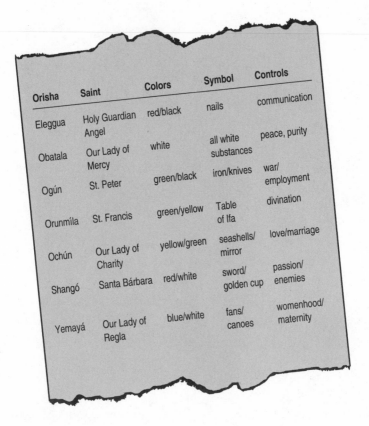

Orisha	Saint	Colors	Symbol	Controls
Eleggua	Holy Guardian Angel	red/black	nails	communication
Obatala	Our Lady of Mercy	white	all white substances	peace, purity
Ogún	St. Peter	green/black	iron/knives	war/employment
Orunmíla	St. Francis	green/yellow	Table of Ifa	divination
Ochún	Our Lady of Charity	yellow/green	seashells/mirror	love/marriage
Shangó	Santa Bárbara	red/white	sword/golden cup	passion/enemies
Yemayá	Our Lady of Regla	blue/white	fans/canoes	womenhood/maternity

Source: Henry J. Krajewski, *Santería in Cuba: Persistence and Change in an Afro-Cuban Religion* (Berkeley: University of California Press, 1961).

4
THE SEVEN AFRICAN POWERS

The *Botánica Yemayá* was located on Southwest Eighth Street, known locally as *Calle Ocho*, the main commercial drag in Little Havana. It was a small, shop-front store situated at one end of a crumbling one-story stucco building with an art deco facade. Its name, painted in pale blue with white trim, covered the entire front window so you couldn't see inside. On the solid wooden door hung a handwritten cardboard sign. *ABIERTO*, open, it read in Spanish.

Miguel pulled the door open to the tinkling of bells, and Vicki stepped in, wearing flip-flops and a short terry-cloth coverup over her bikini. Her red sunglasses with candy-striped keepers dangled from her neck.

"Oh, my gawd," she said breathlessly. "Look at that!" She pointed to a wall where metal cages with chickens, roosters, pigeons and doves were stacked. The cackling and soft cooing of the birds filled the room.

Vicki raised her eyebrows and whispered to Miguel, "Think they sell 'em for sacrificial purposes?"

"I doubt they sell 'em as pets," Miguel said, and paused, expecting her to say something like "totally gross." But she didn't.

They glanced around the cramped, dimly lighted interior. Down the center extending to the rear of the shop was a row of shelves that stopped at a drawn curtain. Shelves also covered the wall opposite the bird cages. Wooden boxes, baskets, large earthen bowls, iron cauldrons, jars and plastic buckets crammed the floor beneath both sets of shelves. They were filled variously with roots, sticks, colored powders, herbs, leaves, nails, rocks, bones, seashells and fresh-cut flowers. Gourd rattles, bunches of chili peppers, strings of garlic, wooden machetes, crosses, crucifixes and bead necklaces hung from the ceiling.

"What a cool place," Vicki said. "Reminds me of a headshop. Don't you think so?"

Miguel looked blankly over at Vicki as she picked up a black rag doll, squeezed it a couple of times then tossed it back on the shelf. She acted as if she were shopping at a boutique in Dadeland Mall, he thought, suddenly irritated. "Not hardly," he muttered icily in response.

For some reason it really bothered him that she could compare this place—where birds were sold for blood sacrifice, where the air of primitive power and sacredness was so heavy it was almost suffocating, at least to him—to a headshop where hippies and headbangers bought incense, love beads and Zig Zag papers. He also was angry at himself for bringing her here; she clearly was an intruder. He was angry that she made him feel embarrassed that part of him could possibly belong to something so strange, so African. And yet, despite his embarrassment, he couldn't deny the feeling of awe and piety, but also of fear, that the room evoked.

Vicki pointed with a dismissive gesture at some plaster and ceramic statues. "Are these saints?" she asked.

Miguel nodded and picked one of the plaster images, turning it from side to side. The saint, a young, angelic-looking woman, was dressed in a white tunic with a red mantle border trimmed in gold. She wore a golden crown. In her right hand she held a golden goblet; with her left hand she supported a long double-bladed sword.

"Santa Bárbara," Miguel announced with a reverence in his voice that surprised even himself. Sheepishly he added, "We have one of these mounted on the wall at home."

Vicki frowned at him suspiciously.

Miguel thought angrily how damn backward and superstitious he must appear to her. But then, she was the one who

was out of place here, not he. "Maybe we better go," he said
abruptly. "Whoever works here must've stepped out."

They glanced around the room.

In the rear of the *botánica*, leaning against the wall next
to the bird cages, an enormous man dressed in a blue embroi-
dered *guayabera* shirt appeared suddenly. His huge, dark face
was expressionless. Miguel and the man stared silently at
each other for a few moments. Then Vicki, in a bright and
cheerful voice, chirped, "Hello, there," waving as she did.

The man continued to stare at them dully. Then he
pushed himself away from the wall and strode back behind
the curtained partition.

"Friendly kind of guy," Vicki said. Miguel looked at her
vacantly.

A mixture of respect, disgust and plain fear flooded him.
Then as if to cast away childhood monsters he said, separat-
ing each word, "What a big fucking dude," and laughed loudly,
stepping back into Vicki's sunlit, if naive world.

"How tall you think he is, six-seven, six-eight?" Vicki wondered, further releasing him from the world where he didn't
belong.

"Easily. He must weigh over 300 pounds."

Miguel and Vicki walked down the aisle a few steps and
stopped before a display of bottled perfumes and aerosol spray
cans—two young tourists from the twentieth century amused
by the offerings of this Afro-Caribbean casbah.

Vicki said, "Here's one called Jinx Remover. The label
says it contains genuine black-cat oil. I mean, *really!*..."

She then read aloud some of the names of the other
potions, each rewarded by Miguel with a peal of laughter:
"Conqueror"; "Fast Money Blessing"; "Do As I Say"; "Voice
Changer"; "I Can, You Can't"; "Come to Me"; "Get a Job."

She paused, smiling. "Now here's one I ought to buy."
Vicki showed it to Miguel. "Stay Young," it read.

"Think of it," he quipped, "eternal youth for only $1.65.
Hey, you could sell boxes of 'em down at the health club. Tell

the old ladies in your aerobic classes that you're really fifty years old...and this stuff is your secret. We could become rich!"

Down the aisle, Miguel picked up a spray can called "The Seven African Powers" and turned it sideways. Now it was his turn. "'Make your petition. Make the Sign of the Cross. Air freshener, deodorizer. This product does not have supernatural powers.' Can you believe it, a disclaimer. Wonder if it has the Good Housekeeping Seal of Approval."

He turned the can upright and looked at the pictures on the front of the can. "*Obatala, Orunmíla, Ochún, Eleggua, Ogún, Yemayá, Shangó,*" he read in a litany the names of the Seven African Powers.

"Hey, the names! The story in the newspaper! Those two gods? *Ogún* and... How'd you pronounce the other one? Ele..."

"*Eleggua,*" he finished. "And the name of this place is..."

"Don't look now," Vicki interrupted, "but our little friend is back."

Again the big man was leaning against the wall, holding a large plastic bottle of Coke. Miguel's mood rapidly ebbed, plunging again into uncertainty. In spite of himself, he moved towards the stranger. He nudged Vicki to follow him.

"You kidding?" she whispered. "No way."

Miguel ignored her and continued forth. As he strode toward the rear of the *botánica*, he became aware of the shorts, tennis shoes without socks and the light-blue and hot-pink "Miami Vice" T-shirt he was wearing. He felt stupid.

The closer he got, the more impressed Miguel was with the man's sheer physical presence. He was like a defensive tackle, really solid for a guy who had to be in his late forties, maybe even fifties.

"How you doing?" Miguel said in English.

The big man just stared at him indifferently.

"*Buenas tardes,*" Miguel offered.

"I speak English fine," the man retorted with dignity.

Miguel grinned awkwardly. He would have preferred to say nothing, but he had to justify his journey to the back of the store. "Mind if I ask you a question about that spray can over there, the one called 'The Seven African Powers?'"

"You *cubano?*"

"*Sí, soy cubano.*"

Now the big man grinned, derisively almost.

Miguel said, "The pictures on the spray can. They're Christian saints. Are they the same...the saints and the gods?"

The man in the blue *guayabera* shrugged his massive shoulders. "You're *cubano* and you don't know about the *orishas*, the African gods, the seven warriors?"

Miguel thought it best to remain silent.

"The saints are like the *orishas*. They disguise the *orishas*. Only they're different."

Miguel's curiosity, his wanting to know something he was supposed to know, opened a floodgate of shame. Meekly, plaintively almost, he fixed his eyes on the giant's eyes and heard himself uttering in a thin voice, "Could you..."

"The saints have power. The *orishas* do, too. Only the African gods like to...dance and eat."

From behind the curtain a telephone rang, and momentarily a woman's voice called in Spanish, "Father, it's Dago."

The big man lumbered toward the curtain, closing it after himself. Miguel made no attempt to move. He'd forgotten that Vicki was there, that Vicki even existed.

"Miguel, you gotta see this," Vicki called out loudly, standing next to the front door and motioning for him to hurry.

Vicki's voice brought Miguel back to reality. He shook his head and walked steadily, though slowly, to the front of the store. Vicki was pointing excitedly at the floor.

On a small white cloth next to a door was a coconut. Cowrie shells were glued to its surface to form eyes, a nose and a gaping mouth. A long partially smoked cigar protruded from the make-believe oral cavity. Before the coconut head someone had placed a bottle of rum, three bananas and a pastry.

"Isn't it darling?" Vicki asked.

"Darling?" Miguel exclaimed incredulously. "Try strange or primitive maybe. But *that* isn't darling, darling," he said testily.

"Well, okay, maybe it's not exactly darling. But…it *is* kind of cute." Vicki toyed with her sunglasses. "It'd go nice by the stereo. Be an interesting conversation piece."

Miguel tried to picture it by her stereo, cigar, rum and all. "Then pick one out. Take it home. Put it wherever."

She planted a quick kiss on his cheek. "You're such a sweetie."

Miguel walked to the back of the shop carrying one of the coconut heads. The big man was standing by the curtain, waiting, still holding the plastic bottle of Coke.

Miguel held out the coconut. "We'd like to buy this."

The man bobbed his huge head up and down and called out, "Ileana," then turned and strolled toward the front of the *botánica*.

"Oh, by the way," Miguel asked, remembering the article in the Herald, "you still sell skulls?"

The man stopped and turned around slowly. His nose flared and his eyes bristled with anger. "You got funny questions for a *cubano*." He scowled, then gestured broadly around the room. "This is all a big joke for you, uh? You think these things are toys? Something you play with, show your friends? Everybody laugh." He suddenly slammed the coke bottle against an empty bird cage. Feathers fluttered to the floor. "I wouldn't take the *orishas* so lightly if I were you, *cubano*."

Miguel could feel his heart pounding. He didn't know what to expect next. Then, for the first time, he saw the big man smile, a broad infectious smile that exposed his gums. Miguel couldn't help but grin in return.

"Is good, uh?"

"What?" Miguel asked, confused.

"Tha' show, 'Miami Vice.'"

Miguel glanced down at his T-shirt. But before he could say anything, a voice behind him said, "Is there something you'd like to buy?"

He turned and faced a strikingly beautiful girl. In one glance he devoured all of her. Young, perhaps her early twenties, but perhaps older; five-five; dark eyes and thick black hair combed straight back. This must be Ileana, he thought. Bright red lipstick, inviting attention to a sensuous mouth; her complexion the color of *café con leche*; a small beauty mark to the right of her upper lip—it moved back and forth as she told Miguel she'd have to get change for his ten-dollar bill.

Miguel stood there amazed as he listened—for the first time in his life, he realized—to the incredible seductiveness and lure of a siren's sweet song. He felt himself blindly, powerfully pulled towards the woman. His eyes followed her hungrily as she made her way to the curtained back room. As she disappeared from his sight, a momentary emptiness, a despair almost, overwhelmed him. But then she was back, walking in long strides, her hips swaying in that fluid way Latin women have, her lithe form gracefully undulating beneath the long black cotton dress she wore, the red sash around her thin waist drawing his attention to the sensuousness of her rounded hips.

She counted out the change, Miguel hanging on to every small gesture. Then, as if waiting for his next move, she began fingering a necklace of yellow and green beads arranged in pairs that disappeared into a plunging cleavage that beckoned to him.

"That's pretty," he said, not knowing what else to say, nodding at the necklace, suddenly aware of the stiffness pushing hard against his shorts.

She smiled beguilingly, not the slightest bit self-conscious. "It's *Ochún's* necklace. Do you really like it?"

"Very much," he lied, not wanting the conversation to end.

"Do you know of *Ochún?*" she asked.

Miguel shook his head, indicating he didn't. "But I'd like to," he quickly added, his eyes big and shining.

She laughed gently. And then their eyes met and embraced for what seemed like a long time. Finally she moved away, gliding past him in slow motion, and disappeared one last time behind the curtain. "*¡Dios mío!*" he muttered under his breath as his heart slowed and he felt himself returning to the real world.

Vicki was half out the door when Miguel got there. He stopped, hand on the door, and looked back at the big man who was still standing by the bird cages.

"Hey," Miguel called out to the giant, "I'll get you one of these T-shirts."

The man grinned, a grin that matched the size of his body.

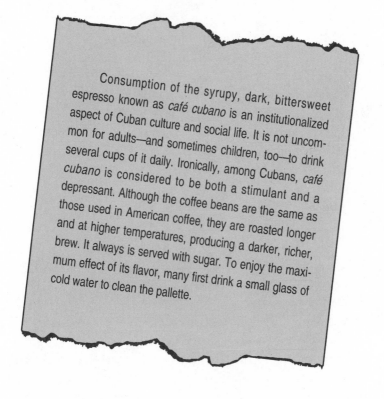

Consumption of the syrupy, dark, bittersweet espresso known as *café cubano* is an institutionalized aspect of Cuban culture and social life. It is not uncommon for adults—and sometimes children, too—to drink several cups of it daily. Ironically, among Cubans, *café cubano* is considered to be both a stimulant and a depressant. Although the coffee beans are the same as those used in American coffee, they are roasted longer and at higher temperatures, producing a darker, richer, brew. It always is served with sugar. To enjoy the maximum effect of its flavor, many first drink a small glass of cold water to clean the pallette.

Terrance Bassett, *Coffees of the World* (New York: The Beverage and Cuisine Press, 1994).

5
COCONUT-HEADED GOD

"What can I say? The guy likes Miami Vice."

Vicki shook her head. "Somehow I just can't see him watching TV. Know what I mean?"

"Yeah, it's like he belongs in another world."

"You really going to buy him a T-shirt?"

Miguel shrugged. "I don't know, maybe. Probably don't make 'em that big anyway. But..." he paused, lost in his thoughts. "I'd like to go there again. I mean, I'd like to talk to the man again, find out some more about this...stuff."

Miguel parked his Datsun 280 Z in the driveway next to Vicki's Honda. He opened the door and had one leg out when Vicki said, "What'd you think of the girl?"

He glanced over at her, trying hard to stay cool, not give his real emotions away. "Oh, sort of strange. Obviously she's into *santería*. Said something about her necklace being *Ochún's*."

"She remind you of Gloria Estefan?"

"The singer? No, not at all." Actually, now that he thought about it, he could see why she might say that. But, no, the girl at the *botánica* was darker and—maybe it was just the ambience of the place—also more mysterious, wilder, Miguel thought, liking the images evoked by those terms.

"Gawd, could you believe the clothes she had on? I mean *nobody* dresses like that. I'm surprised she didn't have a rose in her mouth."

"What do you expect of someone who works in a *botánica*, for Christ sake? They could probably give a shit about fashion," he retorted, a bit of anger in his voice.

"I know, but… Did you think she was pretty?"

Maybe there *was* something to women's intuition after all, Miguel decided. But what he said was, "Nah, not my type."

Vicki didn't appear the slightest bit convinced, but let it pass.

Miguel's house was only a short drive from the *botánica*. His parents had bought the four-bedroom, Spanish-style house with screened patio and a large backyard eight years before when his grandmother had arrived from Cuba after her husband's death. Since both of his parents worked, the old lady had assumed the cooking and housekeeping chores. Although the grandmother had clung to traditional Cuban ways, she'd gradually learned to speak English, mainly from watching soap operas on TV.

"Seems like it always smells this way," Vicki whispered to Miguel as they stepped in the house. "She cook with garlic every day?"

He smiled. "Every day."

"Smells great." Vicki breathed in deeply and noisily, faking pleasure. She didn't really care for Cuban food. Too greasy and fattening, she always told Miguel whenever he suggested they go to a Cuban restaurant for dinner.

"Can you stay and eat?"

"No, not tonight. I've gotta get home and take a shower. I'm starting to feel cruddy." She grimaced then, but in a cute sort of way as if it were funny that she could ever really be cruddy.

"Don't forget this," Miguel said, holding out a bag with the coconut head in it.

Vicki's eyes brightened as she grabbed the bag and peeked inside. "I can't wait to get it home," she said excitedly. "You're such a sweetie, Miguel." She reached up and gave him a quick peck on the cheek. "See ya tomorrow, okay?" She turned to go, then looked back seductively over her shoulder at him. "We can go to my place…."

It was crazy, Miguel decided, but at the moment the thought of being alone with her did absolutely nothing for him.

After Miguel had showered, he headed for the kitchen, dinner waiting on the table. His grandmother sat hunched over a white demitasse cup of espresso coffee. She was a short woman with gray-streaked hair and a fair, almost anemic complexion. She'd smoked heavily all her life. Her face was deeply etched with wrinkles; her deep-set eyes were underlined by large puffy bags. Over the last eight years she'd developed a voracious appetite and had put on a lot of weight. She blamed this on Castro, saying that his food rationing program in Cuba had left her perpetually hungry.

Only picking at his food, Miguel watched his grandmother closely. She looked pathetically old and haggard tonight, and he felt a rush of sorrow for her. He knew she missed Cuba enormously, and that her life here, though comfortable, was difficult for her to accept.

"The *café's* good," the old woman said thoughtfully. "But not as good as what we had in Cuba."

"You say that about everything, Abuela."

"I know, I know I do. It's true just the same. It's not as...*fuerte*," she said, with emphasis on the word meaning strong. "Believe me, Miguel, if you could have known the *café* we had..."

Maybe she was right, he thought. Maybe it's not just nostalgic longing, the wistful dreaming of a displaced old immigrant woman, investing her images of the mother country with qualities it never possessed. Maybe the *café was* better and a lot of other things, too. But he'd never find out. You couldn't go back in time, and Cuba would never be the same as it was before Castro. Somehow that thought saddened him deeply.

Abuela lit up a Marlboro. It was the one thing even she admitted was superior to what she'd had in Cuba. As he watched her, he recalled the time he'd caught her smoking one of his father's cigars. She'd only laughed at his look of dismay and said the aroma reminded her of her husband. It had touched him, though he scarcely remembered his grandfather.

Miguel carried his plate to the counter and got himself a cup of the *café*. He sat back down at the table and took a couple of sips.

"Abuela," he said quietly, swirling the coffee around the little cup, gazing down reflectively into it, "I'd like to tell you about what happened today. See, Vicki and I went into this *botánica*..."

After he'd recounted in detail the events in the *botánica*, the old lady asked only if he'd like some *flan* for dessert. He stared at her a moment, then got up and walked around behind her chair and began to gently massage her shoulders.

"Don't you have anything to say, Abuela? I've heard you speak of *santería* before. Why not now?"

She reached for his hand and guided him to the chair next to her. "Miguelito, it's true I've mentioned certain works I witnessed as a child. But I was very young then. It was when Sara lived with us. She believed in *regla lucumí*, or what they now call *santería*. She gave me a few lessons to protect me by gaining the favor of her black saints. But...I remember little."

"Well, can you tell me the significance of the coconut head?"

"*Eleggua*."

"What?"

"It's the *orisha Eleggua*, the coconut."

Miguel tried to recall what Professor Krajewski had said about the god *Eleggua* in the newspaper article. "Isn't he associated with roads or communications or..."

"He controls the doors and allows other *orishas* to enter and speak. He's kind of like a child, but he has many *echús*, faces. *El diablo* is one *echú*."

"The devil?"

"Yes, that's the worst, of course."

Miguel thought of the coconut-headed *Eleggua* on the floor in the *botánica*. "Then he's kept by doors?"

"Yes, there and bathrooms also. Outside he prefers *caminos*, roads, especially corners. And he likes to eat roosters, *gallos negros*."

"What about rum and cigars?" Miguel asked, remembering what he'd seen at the *botánica*.

"Oh, yes. But that's a treat. Many of the *orishas* smoke and drink. *Shangó*..." the old lady tossed back her head, warming up to the subject. "How that one loves to drink and eat and dance with all his *señoras*! And when I think he dresses up like Santa Bárbara..." Abuela rolled her eyes. "But, watch it, one minute he's laughing and joking, everybody loving him. Then," the grandmother made a gesture with her hand suggesting the violence of a lightning bolt, "angry, very angry. He's the master of lightning. That's why *Shangó* changes so fast. And he has many weapons, many weapons to punish people."

Miguel could tell his grandmother was getting tired, but the subject fascinated him. Subtlely he steered her mood here and there to keep her going. Lost in her memories the old lady smiled.

"*Ochún*, she's the sweet one, very sweet. But cunning, too. She dresses up as Our Lady of Charity, but she's really the mother of love and marriage."

The beautiful girl at the *botánica* rushed into Miguel's mind. "What about someone, a woman, who wears a necklace with yellow and green beads."

"Why, she's a daughter of *Ochún*," the old lady said.

Miguel nodded to himself. So the girl at the *botánica* was a follower of *santería*, a daughter of *Ochún*, goddess of love and marriage. The thought stirred him, causing his face to flush.

Abuela pushed away from the table. "Your parents will be home soon, Miguel. I have to get the *café* ready."

"Just one more question, okay? Have you ever heard of a skull being stolen from a coffin?"

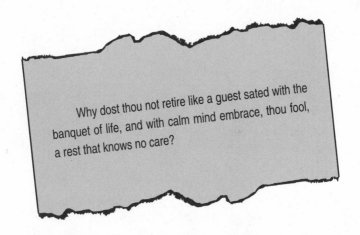

Why dost thou not retire like a guest sated with the banquet of life, and with calm mind embrace, thou fool, a rest that knows no care?

Lucretius, 99-55 B.C.

6
AN OLD COP

The past year in the Miami metropolitan area there had been 663 homicides. This earned the city the dubious distinction of "Murder Capital" of the country. It was not surprising, therefore, for the average age of a Miami policeman to be 25 years, eight months and two days. By all reckoning, Osvaldo Gutiérrez, at 53, was an old cop. In fact, on those occasions when he thought about such things, he realized that he'd *been* a cop longer than the average age of his fellow officers. It wasn't a particularly distressing thought though, since he put little store in averages.

In homicide you dealt in absolutes.

Still, there were times, as indeed there must be times, when careers and life's curious turns give cause for pondering. So when Gutiérrez took stock he usually thought about his retirement, now less than two years away. You'd think after 34 years as a cop—28 in Miami and 6 in Havana, which didn't count toward his pension—he'd be ready to turn in the badge. And, indeed, he was more than ready, and for two very compelling reasons.

It had all come about after he'd been shot for the second time in only three years, and on the recommendation of a childhood friend, César Delacruz, he had decided to convalesce in the Dominican Republic. César had insisted, quite correctly, that he needed to get away and that the island country would remind him of Cuba—"Our Cuba," Delacruz had said, "*la Cuba de ayer*," the Cuba of old. And it had. But for the first few days he had to question whether the trip had been a good idea. In the late-morning hours as he walked through the ancient colonial section of Santo Domingo, even older than Havana, the similarities and differences between the two capital cities had been unsettling, resurrecting bittersweet memories of his past life and country, memories he thought he'd successfully buried. Finally he realized such comparisons were unproductive, and that he'd have to accept the city on its own terms.

Seen through fresh eyes, Santo Domingo opened to him. His daily walks became not only enjoyable but meaningful. For hours at a time Gutiérrez would explore the museums, sit quietly in the cathedral and the old churches, linger around the plazas, browse through the shops and just stroll down the city's busy streets.

In the evenings, after long, leisurely dinners, he found himself drawn to the *Malecón*, the seawall and promenade that borders the Caribbean, where the major resorts, restaurants, nightclubs and outdoor pavilions are located. It was like an unending carnival there, a parade each night of thousands of people and cars, bumper to bumper, creeping along George Washington Boulevard under strings of brightly colored lights hanging from the canopy of banyan trees. Teenage boys, hanging out of their cars, shouted to passing groups of girls who giggled and cast quick, appraising glances at their cruising amorous suitors and then giggled some more and held hands. Older couples, lovers, strolled to the steady, sensual rhythm of waves slapping against the seawall and cuddled on benches, lost in their secret worlds, oblivious to the stream of humanity swirling about them. Shoeshine boys, magicians, peddlers of artificial flowers and vendors of snowcones and balloons worked the crowd. Smoke and the aromatic scents of roasting pork and corn wafted through the humid tropical air and mixed with the joyful bray of Latin brass from countless *merengue* bands. Miami was a thousand miles and another culture away; Havana, gone gray and drab, was decades removed. But yet, for Gutiérrez, its long-lost beauty and gaiety lived on in spirit, here in Santo Domingo.

The first reason why the lieutenant began to consider his retirement at this point became clear during the second week of his stay on the island. Again on the advice of César Delacruz, he decided to buy a couple of tailored suits. You could buy them for one-third of what they cost in Miami. But the savings made little difference to Gutiérrez. He always had lived a frugal life, banked his money and invested wisely, if conservatively. Then, when his wife was killed in an auto accident, the insurance settlement had left him financially secure, well-off, you might even say. In the five years since her death, however, he'd withdrawn almost completely from social activities and dated only infrequently. He'd never considered a second marriage, and clothes were of no importance to him. But his newest suit was six-years old when he was last shot. The bullet had passed through his left bicep cleanly, but it had ripped the sleeve to shreds. It didn't take much for César to convince him that he should take better care of his appearance and that a new suit might well improve his outlook on life. Gutiérrez appreciated the advise and determined it was time for a change.

The tailor, a thin, fastidious little Spaniard, ran a shop on Calle El Conde in the heart of the old quarter of the city. Gutiérrez was immediately impressed by the man's knowledge of materials and styles. It was apparent he took great pride in his work, and Gutiérrez accepted his suggestions without further discussion. During the fitting, as they chatted desultorily about Madrid and local politics, Gutiérrez decided he liked Reynaldo Reyes, the diminutive tailor. Four days later, and one day before his scheduled return flight to Miami, Gutiérrez returned to pick up the two suits. Señor Reyes was busy with another customer, so he took a seat in one of the handsome wooden rocking chairs that populated the waiting room. He'd seen the chairs all over the city and had made arrangements to have one shipped back to Miami. His only other purchase had been an amber necklace and earrings for his daughter, an only child. She was married and lived in Los Angeles.

On an antique table was a dictionary. For no apparent reason he picked it up, sat back down, rocking, and turned straightaway to the word *retiro*, retirement. The first definition held no surprises—"Withdrawal from one's position or occupation or from active working life." But there was a second, one he'd never heard—"A place of seclusion or privacy."

At that precise moment Gutiérrez realized he must retire to this Caribbean city, so much like, and yet so different from, the city of his birth and youth. He could see life coming full-circle, or as close to it as he could get. That was the seclusion or privacy he sought. The mind, he decided, is the ultimate abode for such thoughts.

Over the ensuing three years, Gutiérrez had spent his annual three-week vacation on the island, his most recent trip barely two months before. The previous year he'd bought a large piece of property on a hill overlooking the city. Soon he would build his home. Isabel Reyes, Reynaldo's sister who had studied design at the University of Barcelona and whom he had seen frequently during his last two visits, helped him with the plans. He also had returned each year to Señor Reyes' shop, and now eight tailored suits hung in his closet.

If the first reason for his retirement had dawned on him suddenly and was born of positive sentiments, the second was not. It had been growing for at least five years. Subconsciously mostly, but at times with absolute waking clarity, Lieutenant Gutiérrez, an old cop, had come to detest police work. Accepting this animosity was quite another matter, and he had suppressed the thought vigorously, knowing that such an attitude could lead to mistakes, fatal mistakes even.

On that first return flight from the Dominican Republic, feeling healthy and optimistic, his mind clear and a glass of Jack Daniels in his hand, he confronted the dislike for police work he'd struggled to ignore. Quickly he dismissed the possibility that it had anything to do with his fellow cops. While it was true they were younger than ever before, they remained, for the most part, solid, hardworking, and dedicated to law enforcement. In fact, compared to when he graduated from the Academy, the new cops were better trained and undoubtedly more sensitive to community concerns and, especially, to the rights of suspected criminals. No, he couldn't blame his deteriorating attitude on them.

Of course, police work itself had changed, and many of the changes troubled him. He resented in particular the blatant interference in police matters by politicians, motivated as always by their own self-interests. The court system was another complaint. So many times he'd seen hundreds of man-hours spent and officers putting their lives on the line to bring some scumbag to justice, only to have it pissed away on a legal technicality. The attorneys and judges were always so smug about it. Whose side were they on? That angered and frustrated him. But this wasn't the main cause of his disillusionment. He believed in working within the system—flaws and all—and when one of those child-molesting, old-woman-raping, shoot-you-in-the-face-for-looking-at-me-wrong assholes were put behind bars, the satisfaction outweighed the disappointments.

As the second Jack Daniels dissolved the hollowed cubes of ice in his plastic glass and American Airlines Flight 86 cast a streak of shadow over the northern end of Andros Island in the Bahamas, Gutiérrez considered the root of his problem: The bad guys had gotten worse. He was convinced of it, knew it, had been around long enough to have seen it happen.

Because Gutiérrez accepted the axiom that there was no such thing as a good murder or a good killer, this conclusion disturbed him, although it didn't shake his belief in its veracity. He recognized that vicious criminals who murdered wantonly and with premeditated malice had always existed. He'd met his share. Memories of heinous crimes were the stuff of his nightmares. When Gutiérrez concluded that the bad guys had gotten worse, he wasn't referring to specific acts. It was the collective pattern of crime and criminal behavior that had made him arrive at this opinion. Killings had become not only brutal, but indiscriminate. Human life was inconsequential, utterly meaningless. Innocent people, passersby, infants, literally anyone who had the misfortune of getting in the way was snuffed.

Criminals had changed, too. Sure there were those who had endured lives of poverty and deprivation and turned to crime out of necessity and to improve their lot. And there were others, the mobsters, for example, to whom crime was an institutionalized aspect of their cultural heritage. Of course, society would always be plagued by the crazies, freaks and the criminally insane. But a new breed of criminals, somehow more contemptible in his view, had come to join them. These were men and women, often college-educated and from good families, who held positions of respect and whose lives were enviable for the most part. They formed the elite, were the masterminds in the hierarchy. While their backgrounds varied, their motivation was the same: To exact money, megabucks more precisely, as easily and as quickly as possible. The means to their end was trafficking in drugs.

Gutiérrez despised drugs, their consumption, their ruinous effects on society and the economy, especially this new underworld that trafficked in them. They drove around town in their new Mercedes cars, wearing thousand-dollar suits, expensive sunglasses, gold chains, Rolex watches, huge diamond rings and pretty young women at their sides. The cheapness and seediness of it all disgusted him.

If Gutiérrez could not get to understand the drug trade, it was probably because he couldn't stomach it long enough to objectively investigate its internal workings. And that was a problem, a dangerous problem for a cop in his position, in homicide and in Miami. The experiences he could draw on, the hunches he normally followed, and the persistent devotion to details he had relied upon in the past were rendered useless under this new set of circumstances. The drug business operated according to its own logic, and to understand it you had to go undercover, get inside, be a part of it. He wouldn't do that, couldn't. So he was vulnerable. Drugs had been involved both times he'd been shot, and he'd had enough. Fear wasn't the issue; it wasn't wise to keep on going.

As Flight 86 approached Miami International from the west—the vast expanse of the Everglades below—Gutiérrez pondered as to how he'd tell the Chief of his decision. Drug-related deaths constituted a large segment of the workload in homicide. Perhaps he'd have to ask for a transfer. Maybe he'd have to take a desk job. But probably not. Being an old cop had its advantages.

"You look well, *Oswaldo*," the Chief said to him sincerely. The Anglicized version of his Christian name put Gutiérrez on the alert. "Very well indeed. A new suit, too." He raised his eyebrows approvingly.

"Thanks, Chief, I feel good. Still a little pain, but not bad."

"Then the arm's healing all right, is it? And you've seen the doctor?"

"Yes, this morning. No infection. He said it'd be a while before it's back to full strength. Six or seven weeks, something like that."

Chief William Ramsey was 51, a short, stocky man with a crew cut and a bulldog face, right in keeping with his military bearing. He'd worked his way through the ranks and had been the head man for five years now. A fine Chief, Gutiérrez felt. A cop's cop and a good front man who always held the interests of his men at heart, but was savvy enough to appease the politicians.

"While you were on your R 'n' R...where was it? Puerto Rico?"

"The Dominican Republic."

"Yes, that's right. Anyway, I had my monthly meeting with the Commission. You know how they are, paranoid about negative publicity, the crime rate, drug trafficking, all the refugees... Of course I told 'em we share their concerns and we're doing all we can. All we can, *given* our limited resources that is."

Chief Ramsey leaned forward and smiled. "Gotta stay on their asses for more men and money, right?" He leaned back and continued. "Well, it seems they're suddenly concerned about *santería*. Guess I'm not surprised, really. All those stories in the fucking *Herald*. Listen to these headlines." The Chief opened a folder: "Ten Headless Goats Found in Miami River...Judge Suárez Victim of Santería Curse...Wife Slayer Blames Santería Priest...Mass Killer Medina Shangó Follower."

He closed the folder. "That was the one that got to 'em, the Medina case. How many people that shithole kill, seven, eight?"

"Eight," Gutiérrez responded. "Three in his backyard."

"That's right, in his temple to *Shangó*, whoever that is." The Chief massaged his eyes. "I don't know about all this occult shit, *Oswaldo*, I really don't. I've checked the files. Other than the Medina case and the one you headed up a couple of years ago where that skull was stolen from a coffin and then turned up later at the Sánchez murder, the evidence indicating any *santería* involvement is circumstantial. And I told the Commission that. But...they want a full report. So what can I do?"

He raised his hands in a gesture of helplessness. Then came the clinker of the Chief's whole Oswaldo bit. "I promised 'em a complete investigation by a homicide lieutenant. You can see where I'm leading, can't you, *Oswaldo*? But before you object, just let me add I think you need to stay off the streets a while longer, certainly until that arm heals. I think you can appreciate the position I'm in with the Commission, can't you, *Oswaldo*. I can count on your full cooperation. Can't I?"

Gutiérrez smiled faintly. "Of course, Chief. I'll do what I can."

Walking to the door of the office, Chief Ramsey placed his arm across Gutiérrez's shoulders. "Listen, *Oswaldo*, I don't

want you to get the impression we're putting you out to pas-
ture with this assignment. That's just not the case. I know
how you feel about the drug business. Hell, I feel the same
way. But I also know you'd never ask to be relieved. We're
finally getting the federal help we need—DEA, the Vice Presi-
dent's Task Force on Drug Enforcement, the Coast Guard,
why, even the Navy. And, the younger guys, well, they're more
in tune with that sort of work, grew up with it, for Christ
sake. Except when we really need manpower, I'd just as soon
you stay clear of the drug cases from now on. You've done
more than your share already, and we need your expertise in
all the other damn murders Homicide has to contend with."

"All right, Chief. Whatever you say."

The Chief slapped Gutiérrez on the back. "We really must
do lunch soon. I'd love to hear about that trip of yours to Puerto Rico."

Gutiérrez didn't bother to correct him.

Over the ensuing three months, in preparation for his
report to the Chief on possible links between *santería* and
criminal activity, Gutiérrez reviewed every case in the Department's files that involved the cult. He also consulted
newspaper accounts, articles in scholarly journals, and academic treatises, including a fascinating doctoral dissertation on
santería in Cuba by Henry Krajewski.

His findings must have both relieved and disappointed
the Commission. Less than five percent of the cases involving
santería had resulted in violent crime. Regardless, whenever
any illegal activities were committed and *santería* was even
marginally connected, Gutiérrez was now the first to be noti-
fied. They had made him the resident expert. In that three-
month period Gutiérrez had looked into no less than 287
cases. His efforts had not been wasted, however. The one over-
riding principle he'd discovered in his investigations and
research was that *santería* was bound by ritualistic requirements. Cult practices did not occur haphazardly.

It was for that very reason that Gutiérrez knew a murder would take place. He also knew that it would take place exactly two weeks after the skull of Elizabeth Mary Rolle had been snatched from its grave in the Charlotte Jane Memorial Cemetery.

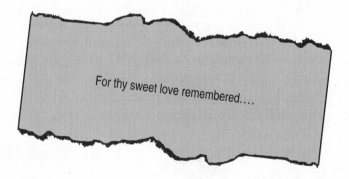

For thy sweet love remembered....

Shakespeare, *Sonnet 29*

7
THE ASSIGNMENT

"I must say, Lieutenant, it's an absolutely fascinating hypothesis. But, in all honesty, I can't recall reading anything in the professional literature that supports it. Of course we academics tend to be interested more in conceptual paradigms than, shall we say, practical issues. Nonetheless, now that I know what you're looking for, rest assured I'll conduct a thorough review of my sources."

"Thank you, Professor, we'd certainly appreciate that." Gutiérrez stood up, took a business card from his wallet and handed it to the professor. "If you find anything that might be useful, give me a call. And again, thanks for your time. You've been most helpful."

"Glad to be of service," the professor said as they shook hands. "I'll get right on that. Fascinating hypothesis, fascinating."

When the door opened, Miguel tossed the copy of *National Geographic* he'd been thumbing on the magazine table and nodded back at the man leaving the professor's office. He was about six-foot with dark, intense eyes and a thin mustache cut Latin style close to his upper lip. Miguel admired the man's clothes. It was uncommon to see anyone at the university dressed in a tailored suit.

DR. HENRY J. KRAJEWSKI, ANTHROPOLOGY the nameplate on the door proclaimed. Miguel knocked twice.

The professor stood and smiled. "Calderón, isn't it? Please, come in." He gestured toward a chair next to his desk.

"I've been hoping you'd stop by, Calderón. Frankly, since the beginning of the semester I've meant to congratulate you on winning that National Hispanic Fellowship. It's quite an honor."

It pleased Miguel that the professor was aware of the award. It had been an unexpected triumph, and had it not come through, he probably would have had to drop out of grad school, at least at "Suntan U." Tuition alone at the University of Miami ran over $15,000 per year.

"Thank you, sir. I was very fortunate."

"Yes, fortunate indeed. But most deserving. All of us on the faculty were impressed with your record as an undergraduate. Your GRE scores were the highest we've seen in years. Well, now you're set. If I remember correctly, the fellowship covers tuition, books, of course, and a monthly stipend of $500. For two years, isn't it?"

"Yes, sir, two years."

The professor's attention shifted to the round wooden pipe holder on his desk with its dozen pipes of various sizes and shapes. He deliberated a few moments, his hand posed over it, deciding which he would choose. Satisfied, he picked out a briar with a large bowl and began to fill it. As he tamped the tobacco lightly with his boney index finger, he seemed lost in his own world. The proverbial pipe-smoking professor, Miguel thought. Krajewski appeared to be in his mid-fifties, maybe a little older, his face birdlike, thin and drawn with tiny darting eyes and a beak of a nose discolored by broken blood vessels. His head was freckled and bald except for a crowning patch of fuzz, and the old clothes hung slackly on his frail body—black slacks and a plain tan shirt without a tie. He was quite a sight.

Waving the cloud of smoke away from his face, Professor Krajewski asked Miguel if he'd given any thought yet to a thesis topic.

The question caught Miguel completely off guard. He knew a thesis was required for the degree. But he'd not even begun to consider a specific topic.

The professor noticed Miguel's uncertainty. "It's never too early," he said. "The thesis can be quite time-consuming. As you know, there's a term paper assignment for my class, the ethnology course you're taking. In the past many of our graduate students have elected to expand term papers into theses. That's one place to start."

"Actually, that's the reason I wanted to see you today," Miguel lied. "I've been searching for a topic, one on some aspect of Cuban culture in this country. Then yesterday I read the story in the paper—the one where they quote you—about the skull that was stolen from the cemetery over in the Grove. And, since you're an authority on the subject, I was thinking maybe a paper on *santería* would be relevant to the course."

"I see," the professor said thoughtfully. "Actually, I've been hoping that one of our better students would express such an interest. It's not only fascinating, but important as well. Yes, it's relevant. Most certainly so."

Miguel grinned. "If you don't mind my asking, sir, how did you become interested?"

Krajewski leaned back in his swivel chair, puffed on his pipe, and began to explain how he'd gone to Cuba in the late fifties to do research for his doctoral dissertation on peasant agricultural economies in the mountains of Oriente Province. Eventually, however, he'd become more interested in *santería*, especially the role it played in the survival of ancient African-isms. "My decision to shift topics was influenced by a talented anthropologist," Krajewski said, his eyes staring absently at the ceiling. "A remarkable young woman, Rosa García-Mesa."

The professor was massaging his eyes, trying to push away a vision from the past. "Rosa had been working as a research assistant for Professor Ortiz, a very distinguished anthropologist at the University of Havana. I'd gone to visit him, hoping he could shed some light on the religion of the villagers in my study area. I knew nothing of *santería* at the time. Ortiz provided some background information. But he believed it was critical that I learn more about the religion, that it would enhance my study by illuminating the cultural context of the villagers. Then, much to my surprise, he suggested that Rosa accompany me back to Oriente. She'd grown up in the area, was well-informed about the religion, and could introduce me to people who might be of help. Her assistance proved invaluable.

"Fortunately," Dr. Krajewski concluded, "my advisor permitted me to change topics. Understand, not everybody would have. In time the dissertation was published by the University of California and received, well...positive...scholarly... reviews."

Krajewski's voice had become softer and trailed off finally as his mind drifted. Oh, Rosa. Rosa, Rosa. My dear sweet Rosa. I can't listen to the old man. Not with you in the room. Your beauty...how it enraptures me! Has anyone ever looked so lovely? So fresh? So winsome? You're smiling at me! I can't believe it. That smile. So radiant. So beguiling! Who can listen to the old man? But wait! What's he saying now? That you should join me? Come back with me to Oriente? I'm afraid to look at you. But I hear you say, "Yes, of course. I'd love to. It's a good idea." My heart rejoices. I look up. You're smiling at me. Yes, radiant, beguiling. But coy, too. As if you were as thrilled as I. Was a man ever more excited? Than I. That day. In Havana.

On the train. To Santiago. We talk. About everything. We laugh gayly. We drink rum from a bottle. You sit so close. I tinge. I feel the heat of your body. I smell the rose water you bathed with. I want you so bad. I ache. It's late now. What will happen? But you call me Henrito. You take my hand! We're in your sleeping car. I tremble. You caress me. You remove my clothes. Then yours. I can feel you. You surround me. Your softness. Your wetness. I'm in you! I'm in you! We're one!

Professor Krajewski shook his head a couple of times, then opened his eyes and tried to focus on Miguel. Finally, his vision clear, Krajewski announces, "There's nothing quite like field work, lad. That is, I mean," he sputters, "as a tool for the advancement of scholarly explanation."

The story had completely captivated Miguel. He loved to hear about Cuba. The Cuba before Castro, of course.

"Now, Calderón, let me ask you this: Have you ever had any personal experiences with *santería*?"

Concisely and as articulately as he could, Miguel related the events of the previous day, including his conversation with his grandmother.

A curious smile contorted the professor's face as he listened. Finally, when Miguel was finished, Krajewski cleared his throat and said, "Yes, this might be a most appropriate topic for you. And maybe your grandmother will be willing to help. She seems quite knowledgable."

After relighting his pipe, the professor continued. "It's quite ironic you should come in today. In fact, the gentleman that was just here"—he glanced down at the business card on his desk—"yes, Lieutenant Gutiérrez, is an expert of sorts on the religion. Not surprisingly, his interest in the subject is, well, specialized, let's say."

So he was a cop, Miguel thought, and dressed like that. But, yeah, he could see it now; there was something about the man's eyes—a kind of hardness, yet sadness—that betrayed the tailored suit.

"Yes, I remember now. In the *Herald* article he said something about the skull showing up again."

The professor paused and arched his eyebrows, then spoke in a lower, conspiratorial voice. "I don't think he'd object to my telling you—since both your concern and mine in these matters is purely academic—that he thinks a pattern exists."

"You mean that the skull might show up again?"

"Yes, precisely. At the scene of a murder, no less. It seems the last time this happened—what? five, six years ago?—the murder was committed exactly two weeks after the stealing of the head."

"But is that enough to establish a pattern?"

"I raised that very point myself," Krajewski said with satisfaction. "But evidently the lieutenant was informed of a similar case up in New Jersey. Union City, I believe he said. In that case the murder occurred two weeks to the day following the grave robbery."

"Drugs?" Miguel asked.

"As a matter of fact, at least one of the victims was involved in drugs. But he doubted the murders were drug related. Funny, though, he told me they found a bag of powdery white substance at the murder scene, which they thought at the time was cocaine. But it turned out to be pulverized eggshells."

"Pulverized eggshells?"

"Right!" the professor giggled in a childish sort of way. "Well, we're getting ahead of ourselves, now, aren't we? You've got a lot of background reading to do. It'll save time if I loan you some of my reference materials on the cult. Let's see what I've got here in the office."

Miguel trailed behind the professor, who ambled long-legged over to the bookcases on the far side of the spacious office. He picked here and there, his birdlike features engrossed in the selection.

"There, that should do for now," Krajewski finally said.

Miguel stared at the foot-high stack of books and journals Krajewski had managed to place on the desk. "Yes, I think it will," Miguel answered with dismay.

The professor nodded his approval and headed back to his chair. "Let's meet again in, say, two weeks, shall we? Of course I'd like a preliminary report at that time. Not too long, ten or twelve pages, typed."

Oh, shit, Miguel thought, two weeks! "No problem," he said. Then he paused for a moment, thinking. "Guess we'll know by then, won't we?"

"What's that, Calderón?"

"If the lieutenant's theory is correct."

Aché is a blessing, a supernatural virtue, a force that can be transmitted from a sacred object to a human being. It offers its recipents both protection and consolation. It can cure illnesses and prevent the spread of disease. Reputedly, it may also function as an aphrodiasiac. Only skilled *santeros*, who know the proper rituals, can administer the transfer of power. *Aché* is found most abundantly in *el monte*, the wilderness, where sacred herbs, known as *ewes*, abound.

J. Merideth Lyons, *The Mythology of Plants* (London: Regency House, Ltd., 1966).

8

CANDYMAN

"Believe what I say, Candy, I know this to be true. I've seen it several times before. The eternal blood of the black saints would course through your veins. You'd have powers you've never dreamed of, never imagined possible, never thought existed. You'd be feared and respected by all, especially your enemies. Think what you could do with all that protection, sweet boy. The world would be yours! And with that face and pretty body, you'd find a *santera* that'd be willing. It'd be easy for you, I know it would. Yes, easy."

Candy leaned against the pitted concrete wall. It was cold and felt good on his bare back, although he knew the relief it offered from the suffocating heat would last only a moment. Through the high, barred window, the late afternoon Cuban sun streamed thickly, and he watched as it illuminated like a spotlight the sunken, toothless face on the bunk across from him, staring with those empty yellow eyes. It was better when he couldn't see the old fag's face, although the sight of his emaciated, tattoo-covered body sickened him as well, lying there in dirty boxer shorts, sweating, stinking, playing with himself.

He looked away. But more out of fright than disgust, frightened that some day he could look as wasted and pathetic as Enrique. But not yet—he still had smooth skin, his hair was thick and dark and he still had his teeth. But yes, someday, if he stayed here in this fucking hellhole as long as Enrique, he too would look wasted and pathetic.

"You could find one, all right," Enrique continued. "But never, never let her know your real intentions. Say only you want to please the black *santos*. Convince her of it. Say the two of you, as lovers, would bring great honor to the *orishas*."

Candy was grateful for one thing. At least Enrique was a good storyteller. There were worse cellmates he could have ended up with at this prison, far worse. In a way, maybe he was lucky. And this was one of his favorite stories, too. He could see himself with all that power, all that protection. And Enrique was right—it would be easy for him, easy to find a *santera* to fuck. If he could only get out of here without losing his hair and his teeth and without his skin rotting away.

"Of course, you'd have to excite her as a woman, too. But you could do that, couldn't you, sweet man, sweet Candyman." Enrique's wet, loose-lip laugh rumbled around the eight-by-ten-foot cell.

Then the metal bunk groaned and Candy heard the old queer's labored breathing as he crawled slowly toward him, whispering.

"That's right, sweet boy, keep your eyes closed and dream, dream of some pretty *santera*. You're unbuttoning her dress. You pull it over her shoulders. It falls to the floor. She steps out of it. Your hands and mouth and your tongue are exploring her body, her soft breasts, her *cocha*. She's giving herself to you, Candy, opening up wide. You want her, want to please her, want to give it to her. You're so ready, Candy, so hard. I knew you could excite her. Oh, yes, that's it..."

Candy bolted out of the king-size bed, sweat dripping from his naked body to the white carpet. In one violent motion he yanked the satin top sheet off the bed, mopped his face with it, then stared blurry-eyed at the green luminous numbers on the clock radio—12:36. Nearly an hour and a half to go, he thought. The peach-colored satin sheet now tied around his waist, he walked to the window of his penthouse suite and looked down 16 stories to Collins Avenue and the circular driveway of the St. Moritz Hotel. "We'll be there at two, *en punto*," Rosa had stressed. "Look for a brown Plymouth."

In the distance, straight up Collins Avenue a mile or so, he could see the lights of the Fountainbleu. That's where he ought to be, he thought. There'd be lots of women there on a Saturday night, blonde *americanas*, hot *latinas*. They'd be sitting around the bar, waiting for a man like him. He'd been there a couple of times before, before he'd started saving money for the *santera*, Rosa. They were smart, those women. They'd know by his style that he was big, that he had money to waste on them. They were all *putas* anyway, the blonde *americanas* especially. Last time he bought two of 'em; they liked it that way, the *putas*. And they liked that cocaine he had, the way they snorted it up their noses and rubbed it around their nipples and down on their *cochas*. They'd do anything for it, especially with a man like him, a man who knew what they wanted, knew how to please 'em. Yeah, that's where he ought to be tonight, up at the Fountainbleu or maybe at the Mutiny; they had lots of *putas* over there, too.

But he would be able to go to those places before long, he thought, maybe even tomorrow, after his initiation into the cult later tonight, and after he'd fucked the *santera*. What a joke, Candy laughed—his initiation into the cult. Shit... But that's the way Rosa wanted it. In fact she had insisted that he'd have to be initiated before they could be lovers. Lovers, haw! Another joke. He was glad it only took one time. That's what Enrique had said—fuck a *santera* one time, and he'd be an *hermano* of the *santos*, a brother of the black saints. And nobody fucked with the black *santos*. They had *aché*, power!

With the satin sheet trailing behind him like a wedding-dress train, Candy walked over to the white wooden end table, picked up a pack of Dunhills and took one out. He thumped the cigarette several times against his left thumbnail, then slouched down on the tropical-print cushion in one of the two rattan chairs. Squinting through the smoke, he reached down and grabbed a brown leather attache case that had been sitting on the floor and tossed it on the bed. He propped his feet up there too, and began rubbing his right foot slowly across the soft leather top of the case. And then, with his big toe, he flipped open the brass latches and kicked open the case.

The $50,000 was neatly arranged in ten stacks of 50 hundred dollar bills.

He stared at the cash, silently blowing perfectly round rings of smoke; it was feat he had mastered in prison. The money, shit, it was nothing, a small price to pay for what he was getting in return—the eternal protection of the black *santos*. And besides, he'd make it up faster than he'd saved this $50,000, much faster now that he'd be an *hermano* of the *santos*. Yeah, it was worth the bucks. And what had he sacrificed? Not much; he'd had only two *putas* in the last six months, and he had to live here at the St. Moritz instead of at the Fountainbleu or in one of those theme suites over at the Mutiny. But that wasn't much to sacrifice, not really, not compared to where he'd spent time. Actually, now looking around the room, he had to admit he sort of liked this place, except there wasn't any room service and no bar and no *putas*. But at night he could walk along the beach and there always would be one of those fag boys there, waiting. They'd do until he had money to waste on the *putas*. Prison had taught him that, and patience, if nothing else.

The crushed cigarette still burning lightly in the heavy clear-glass ashtray on the table, Candy leaned toward the bed, reached in the case under the money and pulled out the Walther 9mm. He admired the gun a moment, tossed it from hand to hand, then tilted his head back, closed his eyes and slowly, heavily, rubbed its blue-steel nose down his stomach and on to his crotch. Maybe he had time for a quick walk along the beach, he thought. No, not tonight! He had to be fresh, ready for the *santera*. Rosa had said they could go to her house right after the ceremony. "*Basta*," enough! he said out loud, then tossed the gun on the bed.

But should he take it with him? Candy wondered. He didn't like to go anywhere without it. It wasn't safe to go out in this country without a gun. He laughed. Rosa had said there'd just be the *santero* and the *babalao*, and of course the two of them. And the ceremony wouldn't take long, then they'd go straight to her house. She was excited, too, she'd told him, anxious for them to become lovers. And, yes, she too thought it would greatly please the *orishas*.

No, Candy concluded, there was no need to take the gun; there'd just be the *santero* and the *babalao* to worry about. And if they should find it somehow, they'd become suspicious, might even stop the ceremony—his initiation into the cult. He didn't want to fuck things up. Not now, not this close.

Candy nodded to himself, then stood. He'd better take a shower, he thought. He wanted to be fresh for the *santera*.

Standing at the door, briefcase in hand, his wet hair combed straight back, smelling of Old Spice, Candy looked back at the room. It hadn't been such a bad place, he had to confess. But, he smiled wickedly, it was time to move on…to the Fountainbleu, baby!

Before the sun rose the next morning, Gutiérrez had found the Candyman's body. It had a doubled-bladed ax buried in its chest.

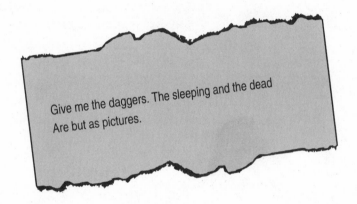

Give me the daggers. The sleeping and the dead
Are but as pictures.

Shakespeare, *Macbeth*

9
DOWNTOWN

It was nothing like he'd expected.

The only time Henry Krajewski had been in a police station was back in Berkeley when he and two of his fraternity brothers were arrested for indecent exposure in a public place (pissing on a car in the stadium parking lot) following the Big Game between Stanford and California. Short of that, his image of what a police station should look like was shaped by movies and police shows on TV. But not even "Hill Street Blues" had adequately prepared him for this scene.

Instead of a gruff, cigar-chomping Sergeant, the female officer at the Police Department reception desk was cute and had been genuinely courteous in directing him to the fifth floor where Homicide was located. There, in a freshly buffed central office area, modern if institutional, the desks neatly arranged in closely-spaced rows, a subdued sense of control prevailed. It was like any city office, Krajewski decided, except most of the personnel wore uniforms and carried sidearms.

Where, he wondered, were the cops frantically racing around shouting "assholes" all the time? Where were the bald, lollypop-sucking, who-loves-ya-babe Kojaks? Where were the defiant, .357 Magnum-wielding-make-my-day Dirty Harrys? Where indeed were the unshaven, bad-ass, curled-lipped hoods, jive-talkin' pimps and smart-mouthed prostitutes prancin' their hot stuff and flirtin' with all the boys in blue?

Professor Krajewski was plainly disappointed.

Lieutenant Gutiérrez had called at 7:00 a.m. and asked if he could come downtown, that he had some photos he wanted him to examine. It was Monday, and he had a lecture at 11 o'clock, but, sure, he told him, he'd be there by nine. The *Herald* spread open on the Formica counter of his breakfast nook, he'd said to Gutiérrez, "I've read the story. Guess it's inappropriate to congratulate you on your theory, given the unfortunate circumstances, I mean." The lieutenant had answered only that he'd seen him in two hours.

Gutiérrez stood at the window of his office and gazed vacantly out across I-95 at the pool-table-flat landscape, the aging Orange Bowl the most prominent landmark in sight. He liked the city from this vantage point. It looked so peaceful, serene almost, all awash in soft pastel colors like a dreamy impressionistic painting. It always impressed him how heavily forested it was, seen from above like this, although you'd never know it from the street. But then there were a lot of obvious things that escaped you when you were so close to it all, unable to gain the advantage of perspective. Perhaps that's why he chose to meet Krajewski here.

"Right on time," Gutiérrez said. "Please, Professor, have a seat."

Krajewski was dressed in black wool slacks, a long-sleeve white shirt and a lime-green bow tie which accentuated his thin-veined neck and protruding Adam's apple. Gutiérrez automatically distrusted anyone who wore bow ties, but somehow the silly thing looked natural on the professor.

Krajewski's tiny black eyes darted nervously around the modest office and settled finally on a map of Santo Domingo which was centered on the wall directly above the lieutenant's desk.

After Gutiérrez had thanked him for coming, Professor Krajewski looked back at the map and said, "I attended a conference in Santo Domingo back when it was Ciudad Trujillo. In fact, General Trujillo himself gave the opening speech. *El Benefactor* they called him. Quite a charismatic fellow. Bit of an egomaniac, though. You've been there?"

"Yes, several times."

"Liked it?"

"I'm going to retire there shortly."

"Oh, I see." The professor looked up at the map again. "I found the poverty depressing, of course. But I must say it's one of the few places in the Caribbean where I think the people actually *like* Americans. Of course, Cuba was like that too, B.C.—before Castro."

Gutiérrez had to smile at the professor's childlike giggle. He's a curious old bird, he thought, but he knows his stuff; the professor's dissertation had impressed him.

"I've come to realize, Professor, that poverty takes many forms."

Krajewski stared at the lieutenant's rugged face, creased with lines of sadness, the thin-cut Latin mustache the only element of flair it seemed to possess. "Yes," he said, "yes, I suppose it does indeed."

Gutiérrez leaned against the desk, arms folded. "Well, I told you my feelings last time that the murder six years ago and the one up in New Jersey had to be related. But I could see your point that the rituals are fairly well-known and the similarities between the two didn't necessarily mean the same murderer was responsible for both. Now...we've got this one, the one Saturday night. There's no doubt about it as far as we're concerned: They're related. The problem is, Professor, that's about the only thing we *are* certain of at this point, except that several people were likely involved in the killings. Worse, we're at a loss for a motive. Unless it's strictly ritualistic and there's no logical motive."

"I'm certainly not aware of a ritual in *santería* that calls for murder," the professor added. "But, I think we should remember the cult's changing, being influenced by a variety of other beliefs, voodoo for example. What about witnesses, fingerprints, other evidence?"

"No, no witnesses." Gutiérrez drummed his fingers on top of the metal desk, thinking. "After the first murder six years ago, we had the lab run an exhaustive battery of tests. I was able to trace a couple of items found at the scene—a rag doll and a wooden cane carved in the shape of a serpent—back to a *botánica* on West Flagler. The owner played dumb and hadn't kept any receipts we could subpoena. So that ended that. Of course, we're running similar tests on the evidence from Saturday night."

"Fingerprints?" the professor said, arching his eyebrows.

"No. In all cases the murderers wore gloves."

Gutiérrez again leaned back against his desk, arms at his sides, fingers twitching methodically, trying to decide how much he should tell the professor. Apparently satisfied, he began. "Sánchez, the first victim six years ago, had entered the country illegally from Colombia. So we didn't have any records on him. He'd only been here a few months, and of course no one knew him, or claimed to. Our subsequent investigation determined that he was involved in drugs, but was strictly small time, a runner probably."

The professor nodded his head knowingly. "I assume he was involved in *santería*."

"He certainly must've been, somehow. But...we didn't find *any* cult items in his house, a little duplex out in Hialeah. That bothered me; it's very unusual. And we only found a couple hundred dollars in cash. That's unusual, too. The guy must have thought he was going to make it big though."

"Why, why do you say that?"

Gutiérrez smiled. "On his dining room table he had a pile of real estate magazines and classified ads with circles drawn around all these million-dollar places for sale—places out in Coral Gables, Key Biscayne, down along Old Cutler."

"Think he was planning on breaking in, stealing something?"

"No," Gutiérrez said. "I think he was just dreaming, dreaming about buying one. Most of these small timers have that mentality, think they're going to become millionaires over night. Of course, some do."

"What about the latest victim, Lieutenant? Have you been able to identify him yet?"

"Yes, we have a positive make. He was a Marielito. Came over in '80 on the boatlift. Evidently jerked right out of prison. One of Fidel's gifts to America. He was another small timer. Name was Xavier Cuevas. But everyone called him by his street name—Candy, Candyman. He was staying in a South Beach hotel, the St. Moritz. Had the penthouse suite no less. But...he didn't have any cult items either. And no cash to speak of, less than fifty bucks in one of his suits. It just doesn't fit. Not at all."

The professor said, "Yes, I see your point. It does seem peculiar that you didn't find any cult paraphernalia."

"And these drug people always keep large sums of cash," Gutiérrez added, staring at the floor, speaking more to himself than the professor. "Well..." He looked up and smiled bleakly. "Perhaps we'll have some answers when all the lab work is finished. There was a lot of evidence that needed to be analyzed. It should only be another day or two."

"On the phone this morning you said you wanted me to examine some photos."

Gutiérrez nodded. "We'd certainly appreciate it."

He pushed away from the desk, bent down and pulled three large manila envelopes from his right desk drawer stamped with the Department's seal. He placed them in front of the professor.

"I'd like you to look through our photos of the three murders, particularly the one Saturday night. I can't tell you exactly what to look for, just anything that seems out of place, odd, anything that doesn't fit. Okay?"

The professor was already putting on his rimless reading glasses. "Yes, okay. I'm anxious to see what you're dealing with here."

Lieutenant Gutiérrez said he was going to step outside for a few moments and asked the professor if he'd like a cup of coffee or a soft drink.

"Coffee, if you don't mind. Thank you. Black, please," Krajewski said.

The top envelope had Saturday's date written in bold print with a red felt pen. Carefully the professor removed the dozen or more 8-by-10 full-color photos and stared intently at the first. Within a matter of seconds his lips drew back, exposing tobacco-stained teeth near the gum line. By the seventh picture—a close-up of the ax sunk five inches deep in the man's smooth, hairless chest, a crusty pool of coagulated blood encircling it—his breakfast of scrambled eggs and ham began to churn. As he tentatively opened the second envelope, foul, gaseous burps erupted from the very pit of his stomach. Glancing at the macabre photos now, he swallowed hard to force down the blob that clogged his constricted throat; he was sorry he'd worn the bow tie. Finally, the last photo in the third envelope turned over, the sour blob lurched quite suddenly to the back of his tongue.

The lime-green bow tie was lying on top of the manila envelopes when Gutiérrez returned, carrying two styrofoam cups of steaming coffee. From across the central office, where he'd stood by the coffee pot, he'd seen the professor hurrying toward the rest rooms down the hall. He wondered if he'd made it.

A few minutes later Krajewski walked in, his face ghost-white and tiny droplets of water beading down his neck, eddying around his protruding Adam's apple and then flowing in spurts down the open collar of his shirt, itself ringed with perspiration strains under the arms.

"You all right?" Gutiérrez asked.

"Yes, yes, I'm feeling much better now. Just needed to rinse my face. Must have been something I ate."

Gutiérrez held up the cup of coffee. "I'll exchange this for a Seven-up or a Coke, if you like."

"No, that's quite all right. Coffee's fine." The professor grimaced as he took a sip. He cleared his throat and said, "I don't envy you your work, sir. Not in the slightest."

"Nor I yours, Professor. The thought of speaking in public terrifies me." For the first time since Krajewski arrived,

Gutiérrez sat in his chair, one of those noisy old wooden models. It creaked as he leaned back. "I know you haven't had much time. But...any observations on the murders?"

"First a question, if I may."

The lieutenant nodded.

"Can you tell me the contents of the iron cauldrons? The ones they used as altars for the goats, and the skulls."

Gutiérrez swiveled around in his chair, removed a folder from a metal file cabinet next to his desk, and noisily flipped through several pages. "Here it is," he said, reading. "Yes, the one Saturday night had a layer of dirt, a dried lizard, a magnet, two horseshoes, seven railroad spikes and a plastic bag of hair, probably human hair." He looked up. "It's all at the lab now. We're running the usual tests."

"I assume the other two cauldrons contained a bag of hair and a magnet as well?"

Not bothering to check the files, Gutiérrez said they did. "Both of them."

The professor shook his head thoughtfully. "And were there other metal objects? Any kind of metal pieces, not just spikes or horseshoes?"

"Right. In Jersey they found paper clips and a brass doorknob. The one here six years ago contained a set of keys. And always there were dried animals—a toad, a snake—buried in the dirt."

"Just as I thought," the professor said with finality. "There appear to be certain general customs that govern the contents of the cauldron in a variety of rituals, including this one it seems. If memory serves, the dirt, for example, must come from a graveyard and has to be gathered at night, but never during a full moon. The magnet, of course, represents natural forces of attraction, while the metal objects symbolize the inability of the person who is being pulled away to resist such powerful energy. The dried animals—reptiles and amphibians actually—are included to propitiate deceased beings, ancestors usually. Remember, Lieutenant, these people are very much concerned with the spirit world; they believe in discarnate survival, life after bodily death. Now the clipped hair means the head is exposed. This enables the spirits to enter the person's mind, the victim's mind, if you will." The professor paused and wiped his neck.

Gutiérrez said, "I'm wondering, Professor. If the metal pieces symbolize the victim, could these things tell us something about that individual, something personal we could use to help establish identity, or motive?"

Professor Krajewski considered the question a moment. "Unfortunately, I don't believe they're chosen that deliberately. It would seem worth investigating though."

Gutiérrez wrote something in the case folder on his lap. "Was there anything else in the photos, regarding the cult I mean, that struck you as unusual?"

Krajewski frowned. "Well, there was one minor detail."
"Yes."

"The cantaloupe. There were watermelons and bananas in all three cases. Those are two of *Shangó's* favorite foods, so nothing surprising there. But in the photos taken Saturday, there also was a cantaloupe cut in half. Only *Yemayá*, goddess of the sea, eats cantaloupe."

"What do you make of it?"

"It must be that the murderer or murderers felt a need to offer food to Yemayá. Why? I couldn't possible answer. Everything else I saw is associated with *Shangó*, including the ax, of course, although it could have been a sword; those two and fire are his usual weapons."

"I hadn't noticed that, Professor. In fact, I wasn't aware cantaloupe is offered to *Yemayá*. Other details?"

"I'm afraid not. Just a question. About the skull... Was it the one stolen two weeks ago?"

Gutiérrez stood. "Yes, we've made a positive identification. I called the family yesterday and spoke to a Mrs. Brown, Queenesther Brown. She indicated they're going to reinter it later in the week."

"I see. Terrible thing to happen."

"Yes, very strange. Well...I've already taken too much of your time, Professor. Again, thank you. You've been most helpful."

The two men shook hands. Gutiérrez noted that the professor's breath smelled of vomit.

"No, Lieutenant, I certainly don't envy your work. Not at all," Krajewski said as he walked out the door. "But since I have a little time left on the parking meter, think I'll look around the building. I haven't been in a police station in decades."

It was not uncommon to find in these house-temples small rag dolls that were dressed in the colors of
the owner's *orisha*. A majority of the respondents (94%)
indicated that the dolls did not actually symbolize the
Yoruba dieties, but rather spirits, usually of their favorite
ancestors. Our survey also revealed house-temples
(6%) where a particular doll represented the owner himself. In the later instance we noted that such claims
were expressed with obvious pride, but the reasons
behind such sentiments were not divulged. In either
case, the dolls are attributed with human characteristics,
and are treated with great affection. Our findings sug-
gest that the dolls' primary symbolic function within the
temple is to distract any evil that may accompany those
who enter the room.

J. Barroso, VIII, and Barbara de la Cruz, "*Santería* House-Temples in
Cuba," *Journal of Caribbean Folk Culture*, Vol. 5, No. 1 (1954), pp. 19-32.

10

ILE DE LAS ORISHAS

The traffic on Coral Way was heavy as Miguel drove toward Westchester and the home of Rosa García-Mesa. Along the strip the signs and neon lighting in the store windows glowed and flashed in bright, garish colors—*"Farmacia Habana," "El Lechonito," "Mercado Cubano," "Joyería."* If you didn't know better, he thought, you'd swear you were in Cuba instead of in the western suburbs of Miami, "the magic city," as it bills itself. It was magic, all right. How the place had changed overnight from a backwater town of slow-movin' Crackers, leather-skinned Jewish retirees and slick New York hustlers to become the extraterritorial capital of Latin America—brassy and flamboyant, self-centered and self-conscious, where the only things heavier than the humidity were the intrigue and violence that hung in the warm tropical air, ready to explode at any moment for whatever reason. Miguel loved Miami. It was his city—part-Latin, part-American, like him, he thought, driving along smiling smugly.

As he turned north at the Westchester Shopping Center onto Galloway Road, the anticipation of meeting Rosa García-Mesa began to mount. Professor Krajewski had said she was a charming woman. And she certainly had sounded friendly enough on the phone.

Past the shopping center and into the quiet residential area, Miguel's train of thought wandered back to the conversation he'd had with the professor on Monday, two days before. He'd read in the paper that morning about the murder late Saturday night and was anxious to speak to Dr. Krajewski about it. He also was curious to see if the professor had read his preliminary report on *santería*, which he'd turned in the preceding Friday.

He had. But they spoke first of the murder.

"Then there must be a pattern," Miguel said.

"Oh, yes. There's no doubt about it. I had the opportunity, you might say, to view the official police photos. This morning, in fact."

Krajewski had highlighted his meeting downtown with Gutiérrez. When he finished, Miguel had said, "I'm surprised I didn't come across any mention of cauldrons in the reading I did for the preliminary report."

The professor had chuckled. "They're often referred to as *prendas*, the cauldrons are. Now...your preliminary report was a good review. But you've got more reading to do. And direct observation as well."

"You mean field work?" Miguel asked.

"Indeed I do. In my opinion it's absolutely essential."

Miguel was thrilled by the prospect. Finally, he thought, a chance for him to go out in the field and do *real* anthropology. That's why he'd gone on to grad school in anthro in the first place—so that he could "do things" instead of just reading about them.

"I hope you don't think it presumptuous of me," Professor Krajewski said, "but I've taken the liberty of arranging a contact for you."

"You have?"

Miguel could scarcely concentrate as the professor told him that after the article on the grave robbery appeared in the *Herald* two weeks before, he'd received a call from Rosa García-Mesa, the woman he'd met in Cuba during the '50s when he was doing research on his dissertation. She had become a professor herself and had taught at the university in Santiago before immigrating to the U.S. in the mid-'60s. They hadn't seen each other in several years. "But," Professor Krajewski concluded, "after I explained your interests in *santería*, she graciously consented to assist you in whatever way she can."

Wondering just what his interests in *santería* were, Miguel asked, "Is she a *santera*?"

"Not really, but she managed to get a lot of firsthand information. She was my guide, so to speak, through the underworld of the African saints. And, I might add, she was quite beautiful as a young woman, quite beautiful indeed. I think you'll find her charming."

The motor running, Miguel checked the address on the house against what he'd written in his appointment book.

Next house down.

He parked, flipped on the car's alarm system, walked across the lawn of an attractive suburban house painted light-yellow with white trim. He pushed the buzzer.

The robust woman who appeared at the door stared at him admiringly for a moment, then extended both hands for him to take. "You must be Miguel. Please, come in. I've been so anxious to meet you. Henry said you were one of the most promising students he'd had in years. I'm delighted this worked out."

Her beaming face and large twinkling brown eyes were irrepressibly friendly. Miguel couldn't help but smile as he thanked her for agreeing to help him on the assignment. Professor Krajewski had said she was a charming woman. Still, she wasn't at all what he'd expected. He guessed she was in her mid-fifties, plump but in a regal, majestic way. Her black shiny hair was pulled back into a small bun on top of her head, which accentuated the roundness of her smooth face. He could see how once she had been quite beautiful, as Dr. Krajewski had put it.

As Rosa released his hands to close and lock the door, Miguel glanced around the living room. There were no *santería* icons in sight. The furnishings—an eclectic mix of wooden antiques, expensive Oriental rugs, Indian artifacts, Mexican tapestries, assorted baskets and pottery, colorful tropical paintings, large floor pillows and stacks upon stacks of books—seemed altogether appropriate for an anthropology professor, Miguel thought.

"Come with me," Rosa said playfully, grabbing his hand and pulling him along after her. "We must greet the masters of the house. They'd be insulted if we delay."

You had to like her, he thought, watching her hips ride up and down easily as she guided him past what he assumed was her bedroom and on to the closed door at the end of the carpeted hallway.

Grandly she swung the door open, dropped his hand, and looked back at him, as a parent might on Christmas morning, waiting expectantly, proudly, for his first reaction.

She smiled approvingly as a look of awe instantly lit his face.

The room was like a primitive African shrine, strange and fantastic. Straw mats covered the floor, and everywhere—in baskets, on the window sills, on tables—were statues and figurines of the *orishas*, some small and delicate, other imposing and fearsome. Against the far corner stood a massive altar heavy with effigies of pagan gods and Catholic saints, a four-foot statue of a black-haired Santa Bárbara at the top, the tip of her crown just grazing the ceiling. Draped from the altar were colorful ribbons, streamers, banners and silk scarves. Leaning against it, and mounted on the walls, were spears, deer antlers, bows and arrows, sugar cane, crosses, a pair of golden swords, a long-handled doubled-edged ax and a white flag. Laid out at the base, encircled by candles, were lavish offerings of fruit, bowls of grain, slices of bread, glasses of colored liquid, bottles of rum, platters of seeds and nuts, pieces of coconuts and several kinds of hard candy.

At Rosa's urging, Miguel stepped in. Although meant perhaps as a careful anthropological display worthy of an ethnology museum, there was a quiet reverential aura to the room, he noticed, as in a church or a cemetery. Dry, dusty-smelling incense meandered slowly about the room in thin, transparent whiffs.

"Come, Miguel, the gods insist on personal attention," Rosa continued in her spirited mood as she began to get in character, as if playing a role. "Let me introduce you to them individually."

Miguel felt suddenly sleepy and imagined he was walking in slow motion as Rosa directed him toward a bench next to the door where there were three icons, a green maraca and a large queen conch shell. He recognized only the coconut-headed *Eleggua*.

"The first to be greeted always," she instructed, "is *Eleggua*."

It pleased Miguel that he at least knew that much.

"He's such a little trickster, that one. He demands more of my attention than all the other *orishas* put together." The tone of her voice and the affectionate expression on her face were motherly. Quickly she reached down, picked up the green maraca and rattled it several times over the preposterous-looking trickster god.

"And this is *Ochosí*," Rosa said, moving on to a statue of a deity armed with bow and arrows. "He's a great hunter and warrior, but he can also divine the future. Of course, *Ochosí's* powers of divination cannot match those of *Orunmila*. He can only use them when Orunmila isn't watching. For *Orunmila*, the future is his own private domain. They're so jealous of each other," Rosa said as if speaking of contrary relatives of hers. "That's why you must keep them on opposite sides of the *Ile*."

"The *Ile*?"

"Yes, the *Ile de las Orishas*—the house of the gods. This room is their *Ile*. This house is theirs as well. I only live here at their bidding, to feed and entertain them," she said with mischief in her voice.

"Then why are they all kept in this one room?"

"I don't keep them," she corrected in the same bright tone. "They allow me to stay here. They prefer to be together so they can keep an eye on one another. And besides that, I think they secretly enjoy each other's company, although they'd never admit it." Rosa laughed heartily and again rattled the green maraca.

"The last of the three sentinels is *Ogún*. He's not very well liked by the other *orishas*, except during times of conflict when he assumes his position as general of the warrior gods. I suppose you could say that like all good leaders he's detached, even aloof at times. But he doesn't care about their affection; he only wants their respect."

After the maraca had been dutifully shaken over the dark, bearded figure, a key in its right hand, Miguel asked Rosa the purpose of the conch shell.

"Oh," she chuckled, "sometimes, especially when its raining, *Eleggua* likes to curl up in there. Of course he has to ask *Yemayá's* permission since she's the owner of all seashells. But she always seems to let him. I'm not sure, but I think he masturbates in there."

Rosa winked as she said that. Miguel laughed out loud at the absurdity of it all, but was still intrigued by this personalizing, this anthropomorphizing of the icons. There were lessons he could learn here. Falling into character himself, he was beginning to assume the persona of a Carlos Castañeda, one of his heroes. But he was learning the baffling ways of sorcery not from the mysterious Yaqui Indian, Don Juan, but from the round-faced and motherly anthropologist, Rosa García-Mesa.

The door bell rang, interrupting Miguel's pleasant musings. Rosa looked at her wristwatch. "That must be my client. He's early. This is the reason I wanted you to come tonight, Miguel. I thought it'd be instructive for you to see a consultation."

"A consultation?" Miguel asked, a baffled expression on his face.

Rosa laughed. "This is all part of a game, Miguel, this consultation business. But remember, people have got to do what they must to survive. Anyway, old beliefs die hard. It should be interesting for you to study how they remain alive among certain people after years of living in a new homeland with a vastly different culture. Observe his reactions," Rosa instructed. "This'll be his first visit. His name is Héctor López. Please, show him into the living room while I change. Introduce yourself as my assistant. Go now," she said as she hurried by him, "and close the door of the *Ile* behind you."

Now I'm her assistant, Miguel mused as he slid back the bolt lock and opened the door. Standing under the bright yellow porch light, baseball cap in hand, was a tiny dark man with drawn cheeks and pronounced Indian features. Quietly, humbly, he introduced himself and asked for the señora. Miguel said he was her assistant and invited López in. After entering the living room, and noticing there were no chairs or couches, Miguel slouched down on one of the large floor pillows. López, however, didn't budge. He just stood there, holding his hat in front of his body with both hands, glancing about the room in quick jerks of his head. He was dressed in old clothes—a striped shirt and plaid polyester pants that were inches too short and revealed soiled white socks drooping about his ankles. In his early forties. An agricultural worker or manual laborer, Miguel guessed.

"Homestead," López said in answer to Miguel's question as to his place of residence. "We live there for six months now." As he spoke, he eyed Miguel guardedly.

From his accent Miguel could tell that López was Mexican.

"If the señora is too busy to see me..."

"No, it's okay," Miguel reassured him. "What do you do down in Homestead?"

"Righ' now we living on the welfare."

The sound of a door closing caused them to look toward the hall. Shortly, Miguel heard the man mutter, "*Madre.*"

The transformation was startling. The hibiscus-draped tropical shift Rosa had been wearing was replaced by a long white heavy cotton robe with a baggy hood pulled low over her face. Only the whites of her eyes were clearly visible. Miguel thought she looked like a Medieval monk.

"*Madre*," Héctor López again whispered.

Pointing down the hall, Rosa said, "The *orishas* await us." They followed her command, López in front, wide-eyed. At the closed door he stopped and looked back.

"Go ahead, Señor López," Rosa urged.

Cautiously, his body posed to flee at a moment's notice, López opened the door of the *Ile* and then froze.

Smiling to himself, Miguel wished he could see the little man's face.

"Go on now," Rosa commanded. "You have nothing to fear from the *orishas*."

López stepped in. Rosa motioned for Miguel to sit next to the three sentinels by the door.

"Please, Señor López, kneel down."

Immediately he dropped to his knees, crossed himself, and bowed his head until it touched the straw mat.

Standing in front of the altar, Rosa intoned, "This, my masters, is Héctor López. He comes to honor you and seek your assistance."

At the mention of his name, López began to tremble. Miguel noticed the soles of the little Mexican's shoes were smooth and paper thin.

Rosa had picked up a wooden platter which held four pieces of coconut. In a comforting voice she said, "Señor López, the *orishas* ask why you require their help. Please, tell them what troubles you."

Slowly his head and shoulders tilted back until his rump rested on his calves. "Señora," he began, "since I firs' heard of the black *santos* I respect them. And never once, not even las' year when I was sick, have I ask for their help. But now," he quivered, "through no fault of my own, I have no work. I been tole the black *santos* can help a man find work. If they only help me this one time..."

Sternly, Rosa said, "You should know, Señor López, that I'm neither a señora nor a *madre*. I'm an *apetebi santera* and daughter of *Shangó*. Even so, I cannot speak for the *orishas* or influence their judgment in any way, and never would I question their wisdom. You have asked for their assistance. They'll convey their *letra*, their message, through the coconuts."

López was nodding as Rosa stepped behind him, knelt down and sat the platter on the mat. She picked up the four cut pieces of coconut and cast them before her as if they were dice. On three pieces the white side was up. She collected them, put them back on the platter, stood up, glanced at Miguel and smiled tentatively. The procedure was repeated, this time in front of López. When all four pieces came up white, Rosa clasped her hands together and said happily, "Señor López. You're a lucky man. The *orishas* have agreed to assist you. Now, I must immediately prepare your offering of thanks."

Quickly she scooped up the pieces of coconut, returned the platter to the spread of offerings at the foot of the altar and left the room, closing the door behind her. López got up, smiling shyly, and walked over to Miguel, who felt curiously as if he too should congratulate the man, but chose not to.

"You goin' to be a *santero*?" López asked.

"I'm only her assistant," he said, evading the question, but thinking he might as well continue with the charade.

López nodded understandingly, then let his deep-set eyes roam from idol to idol. Although obviously still in awe of the surroundings, Miguel thought López appeared relieved, calm even. Coming here was probably his last resort; he must've been desperate. Suddenly Miguel felt a rush of sorrow for the little man with drooping white socks and a faith that his life could somehow improve with two tosses of four coconut chucks.

The door of the *Ile* then swung open, hitting the wall, and in marched Rosa holding a brown paper bag. She walked directly to López and presented it to him, melodramatically,

Miguel thought. But then, he was beginning to realize, theatrics must be a large part of the cult's appeal. Regardless, he found himself struggling to suppress a pang of discomfort. It was all beginning to sound too real. Was Rosa García-Mesa a motherly ex-anthropology professor from Cuba still playing around with research that was her life's passion or maybe, just maybe, an *apetebi santera*, a daughter of *Shangó*? How much could he trust Rosa? he wondered.

Miguel cautioned himself to stay objective.

"This is your offering to the *orishas*," Rosa was saying to López. "In order for it to be accepted, you must drive to the ocean within one hour, no later, and throw it in the sea." She bent down, picked up a glass of water next to the altar, dipped her fingers in it, and flicked them at the bag. "You know about the *derecho*? she questioned.

"*Sí*, I have it here." López reached in his pocket and pulled out a wad of bills. "Was one-hundred dollars, righ'?"

Rosa nodded and took the money. "You must hurry now," she said. "Remember, no later than one hour. Drive straight to the ocean."

"*Sí, señora santera*," he said earnestly. "And *gracias, muchas gracias*."

Rosa took López by the arm and escorted him from the room. Miguel stood and stretched. Christ, a hundred dollars, he thought, a hundred dollars for the *orishas' derecho*, their right. He shook his head and stared at the altar. An eerie, almost tangible feeling crept over him that the black *santos* were leering at him.

As Rosa entered the *Ile*, she pulled the hood from her head and said, quite sincerely, "I'm very happy for Señor López. What this did for him, this thing of the *orishas* favoring him. He was so pitiful, but so deserving. And it all rests on the people's faith. Still, it's not my place to question their beliefs. As long as it works, that's all that matters, Miguel. That's why I accept their *letra*. Otherwise they would begin to doubt."

Miguel's unease disappeared. Feeling an increased famil-
iarity with Rosa after their joint masquerade aimed at Héctor
López, he ventured a question regarding the *letra*, the coconut
divination system.

Rosa became professorial. Gone were both the *santera*
pose and the motherly prankster. There were five positions,
she said. The most favorable was when all four pieces landed
white side up. "That's when the *orishas* are unanimous in
their judgment," Rosa informed him. All dark is a complete
rejection. The answer must be reaffirmed. If the *orishas* are
uncertain, the petitioner must wait a minimum of two weeks
before he can again request their help.

"The coconuts are just for minor works," Rosa continued.
"That's why Señor López was referred to me. Only the
babalaos can read the other divination instruments—the
seashells and the Board of Ifa. They're very complex, with a
different meaning for each possible configuration. It takes
years of training. Of course, women cannot become babalaos."
Miguel noted she said that without the slightest hint of
resentment. Then she added with a mixture of mockery and
pride in her voice. "But I am considered an *apetebi santera*, a
babalao's chief assistant, the highest rank a woman may
attain."

Miguel now began to wonder if Rosa actually worked with
a real *babalao*. And if so, how had she managed all along—as
a scientist—to move among these primitive soothsayers. What
the hell, he thought. Might as well ask her.

"Yes, of course I work with a real *babalao*," Rosa answered. "You'll meet him soon. I told him you'd join us next
Thursday. If you can, I mean. There'll be a ceremony for the
receiving of the *collares*, the necklaces."

"Where?"

"Call me Wednesday evening and I'll give you directions."

Miguel felt uneasy again. The woman is like a prism, he
decided. While she is talking, he is looking at her from all
angles, seeing everything, yet seeing nothing. She's talking

once more in her happy, animated voice about the *orishas*. But this time, despite his interest, Miguel can barely concentrate. He'd had to urinate for nearly an hour, he realized. Finally he asked to use the bathroom and she showed him the way.

Two candles flickered in the darkened bathroom. Miguel reached out blindly until he found the switch. He flipped on the light. A white sheet covered a large mirror on the wall and a pillow case was draped over the smaller mirror on the medicine cabinet. As he closed the door, he spotted a basket of fruit on the floor. Next to it stood a wooden statue. One of the *orishas*, he presumed. He stepped to the toilet, still looking at the statue. His foot hit something hard. Another *Eleggua*, ruler of the crossroads, the trickster god of the coconut head. As he urinated, Miguel had the distinct feeling that the coconut icon with cowry shells for its eyes and mouth was watching him. Self-consciously he felt a few drops of urine dribble on the floor. He bent down to wipe them up with the superstitious guilt of the outsider. As he bent down, several black and white snapshots revealed themselves in the fruit basket. He pulled one out that was sticky with pear goo. It was a faded photo of a man standing by a sugar cane field staring lovingly at a baby cradled in his arms. There was no way of telling for sure. The photo was old, maybe 40 or 50 years old. Was the baby Rosa? he wondered, looking closely at the faded picture. Getting no answers, he tucked it back under the oozing pear and stepped out of the bathroom.

The door to the *Ile* is closed. What's going on? What are those sounds? Those rasping sounds? They aren't human, are they? Get closer. Be quiet. Tiptoe. Put your ear on the door. Listen carefully. Hear anything? Hear

those rasping sounds? Yes, I think so. But not too loud
now. Go ahead. Open the door. Find out what's going
on. Come on. Come on.

Rosa has her back to the door. She holds the green maraca like a scepter. Her eyes are glassed over as in a trance. She
is speaking softly to one of the *orishas*. But no rasping sounds
are audible.

Miguel clears his throat. Rosa turns. The pleasant motherly smile lights her round face. She raises her eyebrows. "The
covered mirrors," she says, reading Miguel's mind. "It's the
orishas. They are vain. When they speak, they demand you
only think of them. Not dwell on your own image."

Miguel just stares at Rosa, wrestling with his own emotions, a combination of fear and utter bewitchment with this
underworld of the African saints, as Professor Krajewski had
called it.

"That room is where my ancestors live. Not here in the
Ile, never."

The prism turns again. Suddenly Rosa is the professor,
learned, explaining with affection to her new pupil the ways of
the *orishas*, finishing the guided tour interrupted by Héctor
López's visit. "Let's see, you've already met *Eleggua, Ochosí*
and *Ogún*..." One by one Miguel is introduced to the rest of
Rosa's *orishas*. She fascinates him with her tales of their
eccentric—at times frightening—behavior. *Shangó* is last,
clearly her favorite. She lavishes praise upon him. Finally,
after endless lauding, she stops. She gently pats a tiny black
rag doll leaning against *Shangó's* feet. "This is me. The
orishas have given me permission to live with them here in
the *Ile*." She reverts to her playful tone. "It's a great privilege
to live in such a holy place."

Miguel has been speechless throughout. He must say
something to the smiling face. Anything. He must come up for

air. Join Rosa's mood. Finally he questions her about the contents of the bag, the offering she'd given López, relieved to have made the transition.

Rosa pauses. She is thinking. "Well, there was ground coffee, plantains, uncooked rice, cantaloupe, honey, a cotton ball and ten cents," she lists as she tries to remember. "Yes, I think that was all," she announces triumphantly.

Miguel frowns, then tries to fake it again, but too late.

"Don't be skeptical, Miguel. Within ten days he'll have a job. He got the reassurance he needed. It's all the power of suggestion. Up here," Rosa says, bringing a finger to her temple.

Miguel reaches the front door. He thanks Rosa. He will call her Wednesday evening.

Taking his hands, she announces warmly, motherly, "Miguel, the ways of the *orishas* are confusing. Even now, after years of study, I'm still learning."

"And by the way, Miguel, the *orishas* like you," Rosa proclaims, her voice full of mischief.

"They do?"

"Yes, very much so. *Eleggua* told me. He's my little tattletale," Rosa says with a chuckle that somehow rings ominously like a sinister cackle in Miguel's ears.

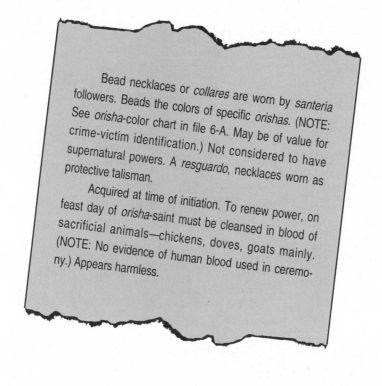

Bead necklaces or *collares* are worn by *santería* followers. Beads the colors of specific *orishas*. (NOTE: See *orisha*-color chart in file 6-A. May be of value for crime-victim identification.) Not considered to have supernatural powers. A *resguardo*, necklaces worn as protective talisman.

Acquired at time of initiation. To renew power, on feast day of *orisha*-saint must be cleansed in blood of sacrificial animals—chickens, doves, goats mainly. (NOTE: No evidence of human blood used in ceremony.) Appears harmless.

Undated note from the files of Lt. Gutiérrez.

11

CEREMONY OF THE COLLARES

There were two listings for Héctor López in the phone directory, but both had Miami addresses. Miguel dialed the operator and obtained a new listing on 304th Terrace. That was in Homestead, a Midwestern-looking agricultural community at the southern end of the county. Mexican field hands, enlisted Air Force personnel, old Southern blacks, young Haitians, and in the winter, snowbirds camped on the margins of the Everglades in crowded, fenced trailer parks rendered it a seedy, but honest place to live.

After a decent and cheap lunch of honey-garlic chicken wings at Tiger Tiger Teahouse on South Dixie Highway, Miguel walked to his car. Spotting a phone booth, he decided to call López on an impulse. It was Thursday, only eight days after the consultation, and although Rosa had said the man would have a job within ten, two days away still, Miguel thought, What the hell?

A woman answered the phone. In the background, children were laughing. The woman responded to Miguel's request with, *"No viene hasta la noche. Está trabajando."* Son of a bitch, he's at work, he mused aloud.

Hanging up the instrument, still shaking his head in disbelief, Miguel stepped in the Datsun, now wondering if he should tell Rosa the good news when he met her tonight at Sewell Park for the necklace ceremony. Turning the ignition, he decided against it. She'll find out soon enough: López will probably become a regular client.

After his call to Rosa the night before, he had to check a Miami street map to find Sewell Park. Turned out it was located near the Orange Bowl, off NW 17th Avenue north of the 836, bordering the south bank of the Miami River. Her instructions were to park as close as he could to the large tree in the parking lot of Dodge Memorial Hospital and wait for her. According to the map, the hospital fronted on the west side of the park.

The Datsun's headlights cast a moving beam along a four-foot chain-link fence in front of the park. This was unknown territory as far as Miguel was concerned. He spotted a sign: Parking Lot Gates Will Be Locked At 7:00 P.M. Around the next bend was Dodge Memorial, a small three-story hospital painted antiseptic white. At the first driveway he turned and immediately saw the tree, a gigantic silk-cotton. He pulled into a space next to the tree, parked and got out. He looked around. The light was dim as it filtered through the heavy foliage. The tree, a *ceiba* in Spanish, was massive. Its fluted trunk at the base was twenty feet wide, Miguel estimated. The roots that spread above-ground like the pods of an octopus stood out a good five feet. He could see why native Arawak Indians that once had populated Cuba had considered it sacred.

A sharp dry whistle startled him into attention. It came from the park. Miguel's eyes searched in vain the forested edge.

Again the whistle. This time a man's dark shadow stepped. It motioned for him to follow. Miguel hesitated; he was suppose to meet Rosa. What the hell was going on? Maybe the park was a hangout for gays. Finally, off to his left a whispered call from the trees urged him to hurry. Cautiously, Miguel walked toward the man. The stranger said nothing. Instead he wheeled around and disappeared into the park. Miguel followed. A pile of rubble stood where the man had vanished. The fence was down. "*Cuidado*," said a voice.

Carefully and laboriously, Miguel picked his way over angular blocks of limestone and asphalt. Then he found himself stepping into total darkness. A hand reached out from the void and grabbed his arm. It was Rosa. There was a man beside her. He was tall and gaunt. For a split second the man stared vacantly at Miguel. Then he resumed his watch over the parking lot.

"I was afraid you'd gotten lost," Rosa said softly. "We're almost ready to begin. It's dark, so watch your step."

With that she turned and headed down a narrow trail, dry leaves and twigs crackling as she walked. Miguel glanced back, and the tall gaunt man waved at him.

The park was shaped like a hardwood hammock. It was a slightly elevated bulge of land, where bushes and vines strangled the multistoried trees that created a natural canopy. In spite of the full moon, the mass of vegetation blocked out all but a diffuse white light. It was like a tropical rain forest, a jungle, smelling richly of decaying organic matter. The air was muggy and still. Mosquitoes buzzed. Miguel thought he and Rosa sounded like a herd of frightened animals crashing wildly through the bush. Instead, they were moving quickly along the winding path that sloped down toward the river.

About thirty feet ahead the trees abruptly gave way to grass. There, just under the cover of the woods, a group of 12 to 15 people, men and women, sat forming a semi-circle. As Miguel and Rosa approached, a few people turned and silently acknowledged their presence. Rosa waved at them conspiratorially. They sat down, five or six feet behind the group. Miguel checked his watch. It was a few seconds before midnight.

"It'll be better if we sit back here," Rosa whispered. "That way I can explain the ceremony."

He noted that her breath smelled of fresh mint.

Soon all heads turned as a shadowy procession of four people stepped in single file down a path that led to the front of the group. At the head of the group was a woman, thirtyish with thick black hair. She wore a blue buttondown dress. A man holding a white dove in each hand followed the woman. Then came another man with a white robe thrown over one shoulder and cradling a wooden bowl. Finally, smiling benevolently, strode a huge man whom Miguel recognized instantly. It was the big guy from the *botánica*, not one you'd easily forget.

Miguel leaned toward Rosa expectantly. "That's the *babalao*," she said, anticipating his question. Miguel flashed on his and Vicki's visit to the *botánica*, the sacrificial animals, the seven African powers, the big man's reaction to his question about the skull, and the girl, Ileana. He couldn't get her off his mind. Every day, every night, images of Ileana bombarded his consciousness, arousing him deeply, personally, in ways he'd never known before. At times he believed he'd only imagined her, as if she were too good—or was it only exotic?—to be real. Whatever, he had no desire to see Vicki. In fact, it dawned on him as he sat there, that he'd gone out of his way to avoid her.

Miguel glanced around the crowd. Could Ileana be here? Not spotting her, he vowed he'd stop by the *botánica* the next day. He had to see her again. It was imperative.

The *babalao* had assumed a position in front of the gathering. He now turned and faced the woman. She wore a serene expression on her face. He raised his arms out straight from the loose-fitting dashiki he wore.

In a slow, deep voice he spoke to her in Spanish. "*Carmina*, soon you will be a daughter of *Obatalá*, father of the *orishas* and son of *Olodumare*. His color is white, because he is the purest of all the *orishas*. On this day, for the rest of your life, the necklace must be cleansed and an offering made in his name. And always celebrate his feast day, for it now is your special day as well. Are you prepared to become *Obatalá's* daughter and live according to his dictates?"

She answered demurely, "I am, Father."

The *babalao* nodded his approval, dropped his arms and whispered to his two assistants, who quickly placed themselves at either side of him. He turned to his right and was presented with one of the doves. He grabbed it across its back, his enormous left hand completely covering its wings. The other assistant, cupping the wooden bowl in both hands, stepped in front, facing him. Even from where he sat, Miguel thought he heard the neck of the dove snap. He watched as the *babalao* crossed himself and began chanting in a guttural-sounding language Miguel had never heard before but assumed was Yoruba.

Rosa tugged at his arm, and he leaned closer. "He's now blessing the necklace, the *collares*," she whispered. "And then there'll be the baptism. It's the start of her new life."

Shortly the chanting stopped and the *babalao* reached daintily into the bowl and pulled out a long white bead necklace. He held it dangling there a moment, blood dripping from it, as the woman stepped over to him and bowed her head slightly. The necklace now draped over her head, the *babalao* ran his hand around the inside of the bowl several times then rubbed it in long strokes over the woman's thick bushy hair. With one hand under her chin, he gently lifted her face, dipped the index finger of his other hand in the bowl, and drew a cross of blood on her forehead. Miguel felt his stomach tighten at the sight. It seemed so pagan, so primitive.

The woman had turned and was walking slowly as in a trance out of the wooded area and down the grassy slope toward the river. The *babalao* motioned for everyone to follow.

Miguel trailed Rosa and the others across the open stretch, which was on the extreme western end of the park and secluded by a cluster of palm trees. Directly across the river he saw a small marina and a new 10-story condo, its bright lights shimmering off the smooth-flowing water. In the distance, downstream a hundred yards or so, he heard the staccato rattle of cars rolling across the NW 17th Avenue Bridge. He tried to imagine what their passengers would think if they knew in the city park below a woman was taking a life-long pact of devotion to an ancient African god, a cross of blood from a white dove smeared on her forehead.

Her back to the river, the white form of the woman stood erect, motionlessly, waiting for the group to assemble. Her eyes appeared glossy and she looked at no one in particular. Again the *babalao* extended his arms out from his sides and nodded to the woman. She turned and faced the water. Her hands were in front of her, but Miguel could see her arms moving. Soon she pulled the dress from her shoulders and arms and let it slip to the ground. Naked, except for the necklace, she stepped out of the dress, bent over and picked it up and tossed it in the river.

She was a skinny woman with boyish hips and hollow buttocks, Miguel noticed, as he watched her step down the bank and wade carefully into the water until she was waist-deep. Slowly, holding her nose, she dipped down completely into the river, then emerged and proceeded to vigorously scrub her hair and face. Soon she turned and splashed toward the bank, the white necklace swinging across her small milky-white sagging breasts and water dripping from a thick patch of pubic hair. The *babalao* stood towering at the water's edge, holding a white robe open with both hands. He slipped it over her head, and she wiped her face on the sleeve.

The *babalao*, who had taken the second dove from his assistant, now handed it flapping and cooing to the woman. With both hands she lifted it to her face, kissed it, then threw it skyward triumphantly. The dove at first fluttered about wildly, then winged noisily at an angle across the river.

The sheer joy on the woman's face was remarkable, Miguel thought. It seemed to belie her education, her family background, her profession. According to Rosa, who had provided Miguel with a running commentary on the woman during the course of the ceremony, Carmina was the daughter of a wealthy Cuban merchant. Her family had lived in a mansion in Miramar, Havana's most elite neighborhood. She had been educated in private schools run by the Sacred Heart nuns. After her studies in liberal arts at the Sorbonne in Paris, she had graduated third in her class from Harvard Law School. She now was one of Miami's most renowned corporate attorneys, specializing in tax law.

The woman had turned and was facing the gathering, smiling radiantly. There was a muffled round of applause, and soon the group was milling about her, offering congratulations. The other women hugged her joyfully. The people were quickly dispersing, walking in twos and threes up the slope toward the trees. Miguel sought out Rosa, who had been talking with a woman she had identified only as the *madrina*.

"I've seen the *babalao* before. In a *botánica* on Calle Ocho," Miguel told Rosa as they climbed back to the top of the park side by side.

"I know," she answered.

He stopped, and his hand went to her arm. "But how..."

"Henry told me," she said matter-of-factly. "And the *babalao* says he remembers your visit, too. That you came with a young woman, a blonde." Rosa gestured with her head toward the area at the edge of the trees where the ceremony had begun. "He'll be waiting up there. He told me he wanted to greet you."

Miguel looked in that direction and thought he could detect the big man, the *babalao*, looming in the shadows. "What do I call him? I mean, how do I address him?"

"By his name," Rosa said simply. "Hernán. Or Señor Guerrero. But please, Miguel, not Señor *Babalao*." She chuckled under her breath good-naturedly.

Walking up the trail alone, having been formally introduced to the *babalao*, Hernán Guerrero, who'd been cryptic in his comments, saying only, "I hear the *orishas* are pleased with you." Miguel thought the jungle passage back to the parking lot and the twentieth century and western civilization was fitting.

Wrapped in a handkerchief and stuffed in the back pocket of his jeans was the dove's head, which he'd picked up while pretending to tie his shoe. Rosa and Hernán were huddled in conversation. Frankly, he didn't know what had compelled him to pick the damn thing up, bloody and light as air in his hand, its tiny brown eyes sparkling like glass beads. In the grassy area along the river he'd seen trash cans that said, Keep Our Park Clean. It was ironic, Miguel thought, how the modernity and order of the United States couldn't keep out something this primitive, this foreign. Maybe man's primeval fears would always be there, seeking explanation and relief, though the means may defy accepted practices.

He stopped suddenly beside a red-barked gumbo limbo tree, shrugged, pulled the handkerchief out of his pocket and threw the dead dove's head in the thicket.

The parking lot, which before had seemed so poorly lighted, now appeared as bright as the lights of the Orange Bowl. Unlocking the car door, and thinking about where he should stop to have a drink before going home, a voice behind him said, "It's a beautiful ceremony. Don't you think so, Miguel?"

He spun around.

Leaning against the giant *ceiba*, the silk-cotton tree, was Ileana, the *babalao's* daughter, smiling at him.

I bet some of you ladies out there talk to your plants, don't you? (Don't worry, I do too. So your secret is safe with me!) Well, you may find it interesting that the followers of *santería* not only talk to plants but also must ask a plant for permission to take from it. Why? Because in this folk religion plants and herbs are believed to have magical power. It's called *aché*, and may be used to protect, fortify, cure and cleanse the faithful. Plants are used in almost every ritual. But because spiritual forces are thought to guard plants, *aché* can only be tapped by following accepted procedures meant to please and appease those forces. The deity that is the owner of plants and wilderness in general is *Osain*, identified with Saint Sylvester. The first step to unleash a plant's strength is to ask *Osain* for his permission to use it. So go ahead and talk to your plants, ladies! And say, Omo Osían when you do.

Excerpt from an Invited Lecture by Prof. Henry J. Krajewski to the Fairchild Tropical Garden Ladies Auxiliary.

12

CHERRY PINK AND APPLE BLOSSOM WHITE

"Yes, it *was* a beautiful ceremony," Miguel said, amused to hear what he was saying, but thinking now that it had been beautiful...in a symbolic, primitive sort of way. "Guess your father told you my name, right?"

Ileana had both hands behind her as she leaned against the tree, her head tilted provocatively, the moon silhouetting the curve of her long neck. "Yes, the *babalao* told me. But Hernán's not my..."

Suddenly a high-pitched noise shrieked from the hospital parking lot through the midnight silence.

In a lunge, Miguel was in the Datsun and hit the switch on the car alarm. It was quiet again, except for the girl's muffled laugh. She watched as he backed out on all fours and stood uneasily, one hand pressed to his forehead.

She walked over. "What happened? You okay?"

He shook his head, trying to clear it. "Yeah, I'm all right. Must've hit the edge of the window. Pretty coordinated, huh?"

Ileana smiled sympathetically, then pulled a Kleenex from her pocket. She stepped up closer and gently removed his hand from his forehead. "It's not too deep," she announced softly, then pressed the tissue firmly against the gash, holding it there to stop the bleeding.

Her calm, self-assured manner impressed Miguel. Soon his eyes wandered down and took in her face, only inches away. She was even more attractive than he remembered, a classic Latin beauty with dark brown eyes, full red lips and long black hair, pulled straight back and then allowed to cascade out in a thick mass of loose curls. And there was the beauty mark at the right corner of her mouth. Miguel thought it gave her a certain vulnerability; it represented a flaw, a slight imperfection.

She was dressed simply tonight, but with more style. Jeans, white tennis shoes and a baggy low-cut sweatshirt that hung loosely over one shoulder. His eyes couldn't help but follow her yellow and green necklace as it plunged into a gaping cleavage.

"There, that should stop it." She removed the Kleenex then dabbed at the cut once more. "Boy, were you fast. Diving in like that..."

He chuckled, imagining the scene from her perspective. "Yeah, guess I was at that."

They both seemed to relax then, and he told her he'd looked for her at the ceremony once he realized who the *babalao* was. She said that she had been asked to serve as a *centinela*, a lookout, but that she had watched it from the trees.

"I was so happy for Carmina," Ileana said sincerely. "Two years ago, when I received the *collares*, it was raining and the water was like ice. *Muy fría.*" She shivered.

Miguel could picture Ileana wading out of the river, cold and naked, goose bumps on her crossed arms, water dripping from those ample breasts, her nipples erect.

Nodding at the necklace, he said, smiling, "So you're a daughter of *Ochún*, goddess of love and marriage."

"And other things, too," she added mischievously, her eyes twinkling. "Rosa told me you've been studying."

He frowned. "You know Rosa?"

"Sure. She and my mother grew up together in Havana, and she was my *madrina*, my godmother, when I received the *collares* of *Ochún.*"

"Small world, huh? And weren't you going to say—before the car alarm went off, I mean—that Hernán's not your real father?"

She stepped back, legs spread, hands on her hips. "Am I so beeg you think I look like Hernán?"

He laughed loudly, glad to see she had a sense of humor.

Ileana went on to explain that Hernán had officiated at the ceremony when she received her necklace, and that she, like most of his followers, called him *padre*, "father," out of respect for his position. "He's like a monsignor or even a bishop," she said.

Miguel noticed that her eyes then veered off to one side, focusing on something behind him. He turned and saw Rosa and Hernán emerge from the park about sixty yards away. He looked over at her, hoping she wouldn't say she had to go.

"Maybe we could stop over at the Café Versalles and have a drink or something to eat. They serve the best *medianoches* in Little Havana. Ever been there?"

She shook her head. "No, but I love *medianoches*. They're my favorite sandwich in all the world." She flung her arms out dramatically.

"Then you can go?"

She glanced up at his forehead and wrinkled her brow. "Maybe that should be cleaned first. And it probably needs some medicine, too. I've got something at home. We could go there, if you like."

He grinned.

"*Bueno.* I'll tell Hernán and Rosa to go on without me."

Miguel watched her walk over to an old brown Plymouth. There the three of them huddled and looked once in his direction, then Ileana came back swaying.

"*Vamos,*" she said.

The towering lights of downtown Miami loomed straight ahead as Miguel swung the Datsun onto the 836 access ramp and floored the accelerator. The Z responded with a start, and in seconds was racing along at 75, 80 miles-per-hour. Ileana glanced over at him then quickly rolled down the window on the passenger's side, tilted her head back, closed her eyes and ran her fingers through her loose curls. Miguel lowered his window as well and the warm night air whipped noisily through the speeding machine, now hitting 90, its engine whining loudly. At 115 mph, Ileana's hair was flying about wildly, and like a kid on a thrill ride at Disney World, she was screaming with unabandoned glee.

The Datsun exited off I-95 at the western edge of downtown, heading into Little Havana on West Flagler, cruising along at the posted speed limit. A light rain had begun to fall and the windshield wipers were on slow speed.

She said, "Since I left Cuba I've only ridden in two cars. And Rosa and Hernán don't drive like you. That's for sure."

"You weren't frightened in the slightest, were you?" he asked.

"Oh, no, I wasn't frightened." She was looking out the window at the sidewalk, where groups of men gathered in twos and threes under the store awnings, hands in their pockets.

"We could have been killed, you know."

She answered nonchalantly. "Yes, but I have no fear of death."

"That's because you believe you'd be saved by the *orishas*, *Ochún* maybe?"

She paused, apparently giving the question serious consideration. "No, they wouldn't do that. It's...it's because I can't die again."

He glanced over at her. Her hair was wind-blown and disheveled. She looked beautiful, wild, like she'd just made passionate love. "I hope you mean that figuratively."

She turned and faced him. Brushing her hair back from her face with both hands, she smiled shyly. "Maybe I didn't say that too well. What I mean is now—since I received the *collares*—my soul will live forever. You know how they say 'born again?' It's like that."

"But that's what Christians believe, too—that your soul lives on."

"Are you a Christian?"

"Sure, I'm Catholic."

"Me, too," she said. "So didn't the priests tell you that you will be happier after you die?"

"Yeah, I guess that's what they taught."

"Then you shouldn't be frightened. You have nothing to fear, right?"

He smiled to himself and muttered, "Shit..."

Miguel killed the engine but left the windshield wipers and headlights on as he peered out the window through the rain at an old two-story white frame house. It had green shutters and trim, and stood by itself at the end of a wide cul-de-sac. Eugenia hedges bordered the structure, and a large banyan tree grew in the front yard. It cast black velvet shadows upon the white walls. He looked over at the girl.

"This it?"

She nodded. "I live in back, behind Hernán's."

He grabbed at an umbrella in the back seat and smiled sheepishly. "Bet we beat 'em here."

His hand slipped around her waist as they hurried along a slick sidewalk that skirted the front of the house and curved around back to a bungalow-style cottage. The porch light was on, shining brightly, attracting a host of fluttering moths. To one side of the cottage stood mango and avocado trees next to a clump of tall banana plants. Clouds of orange and red bougainvillea hung over the low-angled roof reaching down a chimney to a tropical garden thick with ferns and flowers.

Nice, Miguel thought as they stepped up to the small wooden porch. It reminded him of one of those rustic little places in Coconut Grove, the kind that sold for $250,000. Guess that was the difference between the Grove and Little Havana—about $200,000, he said to himself with a chuckle.

Ileana was chanting as she bent over and plucked off a couple of leaves from a potted plant, one of several in a wrought iron stand. Then she stood up again and put one in her mouth. A soothing murmur brought Miguel back from his reverie, "*Omo Osain*." Then the smell of mint hit his nostrils, and Ileana waved a small ruffled green leaf over his lips. "There," she said, gently forcing the herb in Miguel's mouth.

Two delicate white frangipani blossoms float in a bowl of water in the middle of a round wooden table in the tiny kitchen. Miguel looks up and smiles as Ileana focuses the Polaroid.

"There," she says, peeling off the picture and offering him the camera. "Now you take mine."

He glances around the lamplit room. A wooden-bladed ceiling fan stirs the warm air. The house plants wave about lethargically. Like in Rosa's living room, there are pillows and cushions and throw rugs on the polished hardwood floor. No sofa or chairs except for the two at the kitchen table.

"How about over there?" he says, pointing to a large shiny chrome lithograph of Our Lady of Charity, *Ochún*.

She smiles her approval.

The photos don't turn out that great. Hers is underexposed; his has red splashes over his eyes. This excites her anyway. "I want them," she says, then heads for the bedroom, and closes the door behind her.

Miguel slouches down on a floor pillow. A tape of classic Latin dance music is playing. It gives the place an incongruous festive mood. Miguel feels good. Ileana has washed his wound and put a clear thick ointment on the cut. It smells vaguely of licorice. The rum she has brought him helps, too. He's never had it straight and without ice before. Now, after his third drink, it isn't so bad. He swirls the golden liquid around the tumbler and takes another hit. Then he leans his head back on the big pillow with a Persian print and watches the moving ceiling fan and listens appreciatively to the music.

Okay, what now? he thinks. Earlier, when he asked Ileana if she truly believed the *orishas* had supernatural powers, she responded gravely, "Don't ever doubt it, Miguel. I've witnessed their deeds many times." But then with a toss of her head and a whimsical laugh she added, "Of course you know they're all crazy, really crazy. But make them happy and they'll make you happy," she said.

Although she talks freely, answering all his questions, he hasn't asked, and she hasn't volunteered any information, about her past. She says she's been in the country for just over two years, having stayed first with Rosa, her mother's childhood friend, then moving into the bungalow when Hernán bought this property nearly a year before. From the beginning she has worked in the *botánica*. She says it's a good job. It helps people.

Her life is one of seclusion. She has a limited interest in the world around her. She rarely goes shopping, has no TV, listens to the radio only occasionally. She has never read a newspaper. When he asks if she has dated, she answers mysteriously, "No, you couldn't say that exactly." But far from projecting loneliness, Ileana seems genuinely happy, as content perhaps as any person he's ever met.

Miguel polishes off the last of the rum in his glass, not bothering to raise his head off the Persian-print pillow. The brassy refrains of Pérez Prado's "Cherry Pink and Apple Blossom White" catch his ear; he's always liked that tune. It is at once seductive and innocent. Ironically he feels alternately drained and pumped up, physically tired but excited about being with the girl. There is a feeling there, a natural attraction, a curiosity, a need to know her better. He realizes that not once this evening has he thought of Vicki, that he's never felt quite this way about her, and never will.

Miguel senses the bedroom door swinging silently open. He grabs the empty glass resting on his chest and cranes his head in that direction. Ileana is standing before him shyly, girlishly, eyes downcast, one bare foot on top of the other, a knee bent. She's wearing the baggy low-cut baby blue sweatshirt and black bikini panties. He rises, drawn to her, eyes fixed on her legs, better legs than he has suspected, sleek and trim with thin ankles and high calf muscles.

Ileana takes his hand. She leads him into the bedroom, a small feminine room decorated subtly in blacks and yellows with a soft intimate glow about it. She stops by the side of the bed and turns around, faces him, eyes still demurely downcast. He steps up close to her and gently lifts her chin. He slowly brings his mouth toward her slightly parted lips, brushing them, lingering there. Their lips touch lightly. Finally she draws back and sighs. Her breath is warm and moist and heavy with the sweetness of dark rum. His hands reach out to her face, fingertips caressing her, their eyes dreamy with that first look of love. They hold onto that moment a long time until the need to move on overcomes the magic. They are holding each other now, fitting together perfectly, kissing hungrily, tongues searching, exploring.

She is smaller than she appears. Miguel holds her tightly, pulls her body as close to his as he can. Gradually his hands slip under the baby blue sweatshirt and move lightly across the silky softness of her back, unencumbered by a bra. She moans softly when his hands find their way to her breasts. He cups them, squeezes them, his fingers gently pulling on her nipples. Finally she leans back, breaking their embrace, smiles at him sensually, moistens her lips and begins unbuttoning his shirt, kissing his chest as she goes, then sits down on the edge of the bed, looking up at him with those big brown eyes. With one smooth movement she pulls the sweatshirt over her head and lies back, her yellow and green bead necklace hanging across one breast.

Miguel undresses quickly and is with her now, rolling together with her on top of the bed. His face is buried between her heaving breasts, hands roaming urgently over her supple body. She reaches for him, pulls his hardness slowly, lovingly. Soon his mouth has encircled one of her large dark nipples and he is sucking on it noisily while his hands and fingers rub and probe her inner thighs. Her breathing becomes even louder and she quivers as his tongue trails wetly across her stomach and around her navel.

Her back arches high, the black silk bikini panties slide easily off her long legs. He drops them at the foot of the bed. Now on his knees he looks back at her, waiting. Never has he felt such desire. Never has he been so ready.

At last, her legs part wide, she guides him gently home.

Throughout their lovemaking—at first passionate and wild, later drifting and deep, and still later, at the end, wilder, almost violent—they cling to each other. Their bodies and movements are one.

Once he finished, Ileana scrambles off Miguel and out of bed. She reaches down, grabs the black panties from the foot of the bed and begins wiping his still-throbbing penis until it is spent dry. She smiles shyly at his surprise and says, "I just wanted to clean you. Didn't it feel good?"

"Sure, it felt great."

She steps over to him, wet panties in hand, pulls off her necklace and holds it out to him. Then she drapes the *collares* of *Ochún* around his neck.

Walking high on her toes, cat-like, even more graceful and feminine without her clothes on, Ileana walks away. She closes the bathroom door, squats down low, and wipes her moist vagina with her panties thoroughly, deeply. She then opens the cabinet, takes out a jar and stuffs the panties in... on top of the Polaroid photos they took of each other earlier on. She starts to screw on the lid but stops, and smiles. She goes over to a small wicker trash basket and grabs one of the blood-stained tissues Miguel has used to clean the cut on his forehead. She puts it in the jar, too. Now she screws on the lid and puts the jar back in the cabinet.

Lying under the sheet, arms crossed behind his head, Miguel's face beams as Ileana bounds over to the bed. She crawls in with him and snuggles up as close as she can, rubbing his chest and toying with the yellow and green necklace.

"*Otra vez?*" he asks.

She looks up at him, smiling. "Once again? Okay. But first I have to ask you something, Miguel, something that has

Hernán and Rosa worried. I said it was probably nothing
but... Anyway, they want to know why you stole the dove's
head."

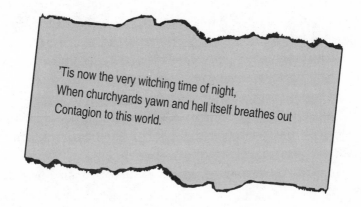

'Tis now the very witching time of night,
When churchyards yawn and hell itself breathes out
Contagion to this world.

Shakespeare, *Hamlet*

13
BRUJOS

In the very pit of his stomach Candy knew the instant he crawled in the backseat of the Plymouth that he should have brought the Walther. But it was too late to think about the gun now. They'd never believe him if he said he'd forgotten something and had to go back to his room. No, he'd have to play along with these fucking *brujos*, not let 'em suspect anything, just smile and act excited. That's it—act. He could do that, that would be easy with these fucking *brujos*, these *santería* wizards. And he could also escape. They didn't know who they were dealing with, didn't know how fast and smart the Candyman was. The Walther would've made him feel better, that's all, but it wasn't necessary. He was okay...as long as he stayed alert and kept an eye on these crazy wizards. Man, just look at `em!

There was Rosa, the *santera* he was going to screw after this crazy initiation, dressed just like a witch in one of those long white robes, babbling on about how happy she was for him and giggling like a young girl when he handed her the briefcase with the money.

And then there were the two priests. Priests! Haw! The one driving was so fat his back covered most of the front seat. And you could tell he was stupid the way he had his big arm stretched out across the seat, steering with one hand and driving real slow looking out the window at everything with this stupid grin on his fat face.

And beside him, hunched down low over at the edge of the seat so that the only thing you could see of him from the back was this pile of kinky hair, the *negrito*. The little black runt had pulled down the sun visor. It had a cracked mirror on it, and he kept staring in it, looking back at the two of them. Candy recognized those eyes; he'd seen crazy eyes like those many times before...at the prison. That's the one he'd have to watch the closest; those eyes didn't fool him.

Rolling slowly across the MacArthur Causeway now, Candy could see the white cruise ships lined up on the other side of Government Cut. Maybe someday he'd take a cruise, go to some place like Puerto Rico. That is, after he'd become an *hermano* of the black *santos* and was making a lot of money. He'd seen "Love Boat" on TV, so he already knew there'd be lots of pretty whores on those cruises. But that was later. Now he wondered where he was going with these crazy *brujos*. It didn't make any difference though, as long as he stayed alert and kept an eye on the black runt.

Passing through the vacant streets of downtown Miami, Candy wondered why they left all those bright lights on when no one was there. They wouldn't do that in Havana. But in Havana there'd be lots of people on the streets at 2 o'clock in the morning, lots of people. They liked to waste money in this country, he concluded. He liked to waste money, too, so this was a good country for him. Before long he'd be wasting lots of money and all the *americanos* would like him because of it. Still, it troubled him that they left all those bright lights on when nobody was there.

As the Plymouth turned on North River Drive, Rosa scooted over closer and fluffed up her robe so that part of it covered his legs and crotch. With her hand under the heavy cloth she began to secretly rub and pull on his cock. "It won't be long now," she whispered. "We're almost there. Then we can be all alone."

Candy was feeling better by the moment. He wondered what she had on under that *bruja* robe.

When they stopped, Rosa and the two priests each pulled on a pair of gloves. Candy didn't like that, not at all. But Rosa quickly assured him that it was required by the *orishas*.

"They're very sensitive to pollution," she said. "But you're not required to wear them because you're still a child in their eyes."

Hernán and Dago, the black dwarf, led the way across the vacant lot toward the wooden shed by the river bank. Candy was glad to see them walking ahead. It was a good sign that they weren't that concerned about him. It didn't look like either of the men was carrying a gun. That was a good sign, too. Maybe things here were okay. Maybe these *brujos* really believed all their witchcraft. Maybe there really was something in all this for him, being an *hermano* of the *santos*. Candy grew excited.

Dago stepped in the shed first. Hernán followed him and closed the door behind him. Rosa reached over and tugged on Candy's arm with both hands. She kissed him on the cheek. "It's a simple ceremony and it won't take long, you'll see." Candy was thinking it wouldn't be quick enough for him.

In the dim red glow that barely illuminated the hot little building, Candy spotted several chickens and a goat. They were walking in circles over in the opposite corner from where the two priests were squatting down lighting candles. Candy took in the room with a few quick glances. His eyes came to rest finally on a small darkened object sitting in the middle of a wooden shelf against the far wall. He batted his eyes and squinted. Yes, it was a skull all right. Once again he felt something twist in the pit of his stomach. Clumsily he spun around and faced the other three, all standing together now. He batted his eyes again.

It was extraordinary how the light from a single votive candle could glint so brilliantly off the blade of a machete.

Lieutenant Gutiérrez had his favorite restaurants, all of which happened to be Cuban. It wasn't that he didn't like other cuisines. Occasionally he truly enjoyed a good French meal, and sometimes he even craved Chinese. Then, during the winter, he looked forward to stone crabs and key lime pie, specially from Joe's Stone Crab on Miami Beach. But the Cuban restaurants had something the other places lacked— an atmosphere he felt comfortable in. And that, the ambience, was more important to him than the food itself.

Not that all Cuban restaurants were alike. On days when he missed the island the most, he wanted to be around his compatriots in a joyful place, a place suspended in time, a place like old Havana or as close as you could get to it. Then he would dine at La Esquina de Tejas, La Carreta or La Tasca. When he craved something more elegant and subdued, he favored El Cid. Today, he needed a restaurant where he could relax and think, uninterrupted by the din of conversation or the doting waiters. But not wanting a place so quiet he would feel self-conscious, he decided on Malaga, an attractive little Spanish-Cuban establishment on *Calle Ocho* that served the best black bean soup in town.

Now, as he dipped into the thick, chocolate-colored soup, Gutiérrez pondered the murder of Xavier "Candy" Cuevas. His meeting at the medical examiner's office, over two weeks before, was raising more questions than providing answers. The cause of death did not trouble him. It had come about as a result of a single "extraordinarily forceful" blow that penetrated the chest cavity 14 centimeters and had severed the heart in the process, causing instant death. Such was the report of the deputy medical examiner, a nervous little man named Ira Goldbaum.

"We were somewhat surprised that there were no hand or arm wounds," Goldbaum had said. "Usually in a murder of this kind the victim attempts to block the blows. But that's not the case here. We suspect he didn't know he was about to be axed or..."

Gutiérrez interrupted. "You mean that he was blindfolded or hooded perhaps, something like that?"

"Yes, I'd suspect so."

"Which means then that he must have been held against his will, or else he trusted the murderer, or murderers."

Goldbaum nodded. "Or...he willingly offered himself as sacrifice. Of course, I can't fathom anyone doing that but, well, this *is* Miami and we've seen stranger things in *this* Department."

Gutiérrez wondered what would compel a man to become a medical examiner, a coroner as they used to be called. Looking around the morgue, the shiny tiles and stainless steel belying the rot and decay they reflected every day, he said, "Yes, I imagine so."

The deputy medical examiner noticed the expression of empathy, or at least what he interpreted to be empathy. "Not that you haven't seen your share, Lieutenant. In fact, I remember some of your cases, the Medina murders in particular. I was new in the Department at the time, and those were the first cult killings—I guess you could call 'em that—I worked on. Awful messy job, awful messy."

Gutiérrez agreed, recalling the three butchered victims slaughtered before a crude altar to *Shangó*.

"There was something else about this Cuevas murder we think you might find interesting."

Gutiérrez looked over at Goldbaum and thought he detected a thin smile forming on the usually dead-serious face. "What's that?"

"Let me ask you first, when you discovered the body did you notice the victim's pants?"

Closing his eyes, Gutiérrez revisited the murder scene as he had a hundred times before. "No, I don't remember anything unusual."

"Well, they were unzipped. And, it turns out, there were traces of semen on them and on his shorts. Not much, like the guy had a preejaculatory discharge. So he must have had an erection sometime prior to his death."

Gutiérrez took a bite of the crusty bread drenched in gar-
lic-butter they served with the soup. If he were at home he
would have dunked it in the bowl and sopped up the last of
the broth. But not here. He was a man who believed in deco-
rum. His second glass of white Spanish wine in hand, he considered again the possible sexual dimension of the murder.
While lascivious behavior was not unusual in *santería* rituals,
it typically was confined to salacious gestures, executed more
for their symbolic value than out of real sexual intent. In all of
his experiences with the cult, he could think of only two—or
was it three?—cases where ceremonies had included explicit
sexual acts. He had read, however, that in Africa copulation
rituals were common. In the two related cases—the one in
Miami six years ago, and the one up in New Jersey—no evidence supported a sexual component. But that in itself did not
rule out the possibility. Evidence, as Gutiérrez well knew, was
like statistics. It told only half the story.

Regardless, this was an aspect of the case which had to be
considered. The possibility existed that the guy simply got
excited about the ceremony and cummed in his drawers. Since
there had been no apparent physical torture, he dismissed
masochism. He did not eliminate sadism, however. After all,
to a hardcore sadist, a snuff job would seem to be the ultimate
thrill.

A possible homosexual tie had not escaped him either.
Yet, while these deviant activities were all within the realm of
possibility, what Gutiérrez concluded was that the semen
stains present increased the probability that a woman was
present at the murder scene and could have played an active
role in it.

Gutiérrez considered having another glass of wine. But he
checked the time and ordered a cup of *café cubano* instead. He
was to meet with Queenesther Brown, the daughter of Mary
Elizabeth Rolle, at her home in Coconut Grove in twenty minutes. It was a meeting he'd dreaded all morning. When Mrs.
Brown had called yesterday, she said only that she wanted to

talk with Gutiérrez. He hadn't pressed her as to what the motive might be. And while she had sounded friendly enough on the phone, he wouldn't be a bit surprised if she planned on using this meeting to vent her frustrations and anger over the theft of her mother's skull. The families of crime victims, he'd learned, often wanted to blame the Department; it was something he'd dealt with many times before. Of course, there was always the possibility that she might have something positive to contribute to the investigation, and that, if nothing else, made it worth the time. But still, he had dreaded the meeting all morning.

Queenesther Brown's house was on historic Charles Avenue in the heart of the black Grove, directly across the narrow tree-lined street from the Charlotte Jane Memorial Cemetery. Gutiérrez parked the Ford and walked up the steps of the old frame house with bright pink wooden shutters. Four rickety chairs lined the small front porch.

He was about to knock when a young teenage boy dressed in cut-off shorts, white tank top and a gold chain came out the open door, stopped abruptly, and gave him a defiant once-over. Gutiérrez asked if Mrs. Brown was home.

"Moma, the man's here," he called out, his eyes still fixed on Gutiérrez, now coldly appraising his suit. It never ceased to impress the lieutenant how blacks of all ages could always finger a cop. For that very reason, during his earlier years on the force he'd hated working vice in the ghetto. Apparently satisfied, the boy nodded slowly and muttered, "Least you wear some rags, for a police."

Gutiérrez smiled as a stunningly handsome, light-skinned black woman about thirty-five years old appeared at the door. She smoothed out her dress before extending her limp, delicate hand to thank him for coming.

Already he felt better about the prospects of this meeting.

"I'm goin' over to Peacock Park," the boy said, heading down the steps.

"Just you be back for supper," the woman said. "You hear, Marcus?"

"You know I ain't gonna miss no supper," he replied, looking back at her and grinning.

As Gutiérrez and the woman entered the house, a voice from across the cramped but neat little living room said, "You're late, seven minutes late." The lieutenant's eyes focused on a rail-thin boy of about eight or nine who was pointing at a beautiful hand-polished mantel clock.

"Billy!" the mother said empathically, putting her wrists on her hips and giving the child a tired look. "You just go on about your own business and give us some peace and quiet around here. Go on now, honey." Billy dragged his feet as she shooed him out of the room.

"Kids..." the woman said to Gutiérrez, smiling motherly and motioning for him to have a seat on the couch. "He learnt to tell time at school this year and he's so proud of hisself."

"Well, he's right. I am late." Queenesther eased down next to him and crossed her legs. Befitting her name, she was endowed with natural feminine elegance.

"I want you to know, Mrs. Brown, how much we all regret this crazy thing that happened to your family. If we can be of any help..."

The woman reached over and lightly touched the sleeve of Gutiérrez's suit. He noticed that the nails of her long brown fingers were painted a glossy ruby-red. "You people have been very kind to us. We was all surprised how nice you've been. It's just that, well, now that Moma's been properly buried again, we was wonderin' if you've given up on findin' them crazy voodoo people who violated her grave like that?"

"Certainly not, Mrs. Brown. The case is still very much under investigation. Unfortunately, as you know, it's linked to a murder, so we're doing all we can to solve it."

"You have ideas who done it?"

"We have several leads we're working on."

Queenesther got up and walked slowly over to the mantel clock, tapped it a couple of times and turned back toward the lieutenant. "This is probably nothing, just a child's 'magination. But Billy keeps sayin' it's so."

"What's that, Mrs. Brown?"

"That he saw them voodoo people 'cross the street the night Moma's grave was violated. He said he saw a giant, and a dwarf, and a ghost. He kept saying it and saying it. But you know how kids dream up things."

"Does Billy often dream up things?"

"No more than most little boys. Less than Marcus did when he was Billy's age, that's for sure. I figured it was just because of all that happened. But he kept sayin' it and sayin' it."

"Did Billy say what they were doing, the voodoo people?"

"Said he saw 'em when they was leavin' and it was lightning. The giant was draggin' a big bag like Santa Claus has, and the ghost was carrying something round. I guess that would be my Moma's head." The woman looked at Gutiérrez and let her shoulders slump.

He gave her a sympathetic look. "I know this has been difficult on you, Mrs. Brown. Understand how much we appreciate your cooperation. This new...information could be valuable to our investigation. But, if I may ask, why did you wait until now to tell us what Billy saw?"

"Well, after a while he finally stopped talkin' about it so much, and we thought it was over and done with. Then, sure enough, he said he saw 'em again. Only this time there was just two—the ghost and a regular man. The giant and the dwarf weren't with 'em."

"And when was that, Mrs. Brown? When did he say he saw them, the ghost and the regular man?"

She paused, looking up at the ceiling. "Seems like it was just before, maybe two or three days before they called and said they found Moma's head."

Gutiérrez calculated the dates. Yes, it would be the night Xavier "Candy" Cuevas was murdered. "Mrs. Brown, I'm curious why Billy would be up so late at night."

"He don't sleep so good anyway. When it's thunderin' and lightnin' out he likes to come out here and stay on the couch."

"Why do you suppose he thought it was a ghost he saw?"

"'Cause it was all white."

"I see. Did he say what the ghost and the regular man were doing?"

"Only that they was there, over by Moma's grave, for a minute or two and they was pickin' up something from the ground, but he didn't know what. Next day I went over there myself, but I didn't see nothin' wrong."

"Did Billy say anything about the regular man, like what he was wearing or who was taller, he or the ghost?"

From across the room, his face peering around the door, Billy called out, "The man was taller, but he weren't no giant."

The woman spun around and faced the child, wrists on her hips again. "Didn't Moma tell you to get on about your own business, mister? Now you get in that room and stay there, 'fore I get mad."

"Oh, Moma, I was just…"

Gutiérrez said, "Mrs. Brown, do you mind if I ask Billy a question?"

She frowned at the boy but said, "I guess it ain't gonna hurt nothin' now."

"Billy, when you saw the ghost and the regular man, did you happen to notice what time it was?"

"I always look at the clock when them voodoo people come around. It was 3:06 in the mornin'. Marcus say you don't gotta worry 'less they come at midnight. Then you gotta look out, boy."

Lieutenant Gutiérrez smiled.

The sacred drums of *santería* talk. That's right. The *batás*, as they're called, hold six-handed conversations. Each of the *orishas*, you see, has its own beat, its own rhythmic structure. So when the *batás* play an *orisha's* beat, they are conversing with it, asking it to come down, to speak, to share its wisdom. Why a six-handed conversation? Because there are three drums, with two sides each. The two-headed, goblet-shaped drums are held across the drummers' laps, the largest of the drumheads on the players' right side. The biggest of the three drums—the *iya*—is the bass. It sets the tempo for the two smaller drums, the *itotele* and the *konkolo*. Although each drum has its own distinctive sound, the trio fuses into a cohesive ensemble that makes musical and ritual sense only when considered as a whole.

The drummers are called *oloris*. It takes years of dedicated training to play the *batás*. Consequently, there are not many *oloris* around. So today, most of the ceremonies that call for the *batás* use only records of *batá* music. Only men can become *oloris*. Not only that, women cannot even touch the sacred drums. Why? Because the Yorubas, like most African tribes, believe women's menstrual cycles drain them of strength, and is a sign of impurity.

In the Yoruba belief system, the *batás* are considered very susceptible to pollution.

Excerpted from a guest lecture by Prof. Henry J. Krajewski to Prof. Richard Rose's ethnomusicology course, Miami-Dade Community College.

14
JUNGLE DREAMS

"You bet we got 'em. What size?"

Miguel was perplexed. "Gee, I don't know exactly. Extra large, for sure."

The clerk chuckled. "All of our shirts are extra large, you might say."

Miguel had driven by the Big and Tall store at Coral Reef and South Dixie a thousand times before and had always been curious about the place with its sign out front that said, "Perfect Fits for Talls and Bigs." But never once had he thought about how sizes for bigs and talls ran.

"Is the gentleman over six-foot?"

"Oh yeah, he's about six-seven, six-eight."

"About as tall as me?"

Miguel sized up the freckled-faced, red-headed clerk. "I'd say he's at least your height."

"Okay, let's say six-eight. And he weighs?"

"Around 300, maybe 320."

"Fine, a 3-X-T should do nicely. They're right over here."

Miguel tossed the bag on the back seat of the Datsun and headed up the highway toward Ileana's. Later in the evening they were going to a ceremony, the *santos subidos*, the descending of the saints. It was a ceremony Ileana had assured him he would enjoy, with lots of food and drumming and dancing and singing. "And when the *orishas* mount their horses," she'd added excitedly, "that's when the fun begins."

Rosa and Hernán were just climbing out of the Plymouth when Miguel and Ileana pulled in the darkened parking lot of what appeared to be an abandoned warehouse somewhere in the industrial district of Hialeah. Rosa hurried over to them. She first hugged Ileana, then took Miguel's hands and held them at arm's length. "This is an important experience in your continuing education, Miguel," she said, assuming her professorial stance. "Tonight you'll have the honor of actually *seeing* the *orishas!*"

In truth, he *was* excited about the evening's prospects. Trance possession was one of the cult's practices which he'd found particularly fascinating in his readings. He also was more than a little relieved that Rosa had greeted them in such a warm and receptive manner. Even though he'd been with Ileana virtually every night since the initiation nearly two weeks ago, he'd spoken with Rosa and Hernán only once during that time. That had been last Saturday night when the two of them happened to be coming out the back door of Hernán's as he was rounding the path to Ileana's bungalow. The attachment he sensed between the Cuban anthropologist and the *babalao* was beginning to worry him.

Rosa had wasted little time on formalities. "I assume you know, Miguel, that Hernán is concerned over that incident with the dove's head. Such a foolish act he feels could have led to the gravest of consequences, especially for the new devotee."

Miguel was relieved tonight that things seemed, ostensibly, okay.

"I have something for you," he said to Hernán, holding out the bag.

Hernán took it tentatively and peered inside big-eyed. Slowly, as he pulled out the black T-shirt with "Miami" written in aqua blue and "Vice" in hot pink, a gargantuan grin contorted his huge face.

"*¡Qué bueno!*" he exclaimed, reaching out and patting Miguel's shoulder. "*Gracias, mil gracias.* I bet it will please *Yemayá* if I wear this tonight. I know what she likes."

Ileana and Miguel smiled at each other as Hernán quickly unbuttoned his *guayabera* and handed it to Rosa, who sniffed condescendingly as she took it. Covering Hernán's mammoth chest and stomach was an exquisite tattoo of *Yemayá*, goddess of the sea, with three men in a boat looking up reverently at their patroness. It was the biggest tattoo Miguel had ever seen.

The T-shirt on, Hernán looked over at them and beamed. If he hadn't worn his pants so low, Miguel thought, it would almost fit him. Ileana giggled and said how much she liked it. Rosa shook her head disgustedly.

After climbing a short flight of stairs to a cement loading dock on the back of the building, they were met by a man called Geraldo. He escorted them to a large sliding door that he pulled open with both hands, but only wide enough to allow one person at a time to enter.

Just inside the doorway stood an elderly woman. She was puffing on a cigar. As they stepped in, one by one, the woman blew smoke in their faces. She repeated the word "*Lacumí*" in a raspy voice. Miguel wasn't overly surprised. He had read that cigar smoke is used often to symbolically purify participants before certain ceremonies. And that in Yoruba the term *lacumí* means my friend or friend of the *orishas*.

As they approached the group, Miguel estimated there were about 35 or 40 people milling around several long tables covered with food and drinks. They were talking in loud, animated voices which echoed off the high ceiling and barren walls of the otherwise empty structure. Unlike the solemnity of the initiation, the mood tonight was jovial and festive. It seemed to Miguel to be less a ceremony than a celebration, a party. Well-wishers immediately surrounded Rosa and Hernán as they began their rounds, greeting everyone warmly and calling each by name.

"They remind me of priests at a parish social," he remarked to Ileana, who was waving to two women by the end of the food tables.

She answered matter-of-factly. "They are priests, Miguel. Now come on, I want you to meet Carmina, the woman who was initiated. And then let's eat. I'm starving."

He scarcely recognized the woman who only two weeks ago on the banks of the Miami River had become a daughter of *Obatalá*. With her hair pulled back and her make-up on and the way she was dressed tonight—in tight black designer pants and an elegant long-sleeve ivory-colored silk blouse— she appeared ten years younger. Even so, as Ileana introduced them, he couldn't erase the image of her wading zombie-like out of the river, her little tits sagging and water dripping from that thick jungle of pubic hair.

"I'm very happy to meet you," Carmina said. "Ileana was like a sister to me when I was preparing to receive the *collares*. She's a very special person. But you know that, don't you?" Ileana and Carmina then hugged, cheek to cheek, kissing the air. Turning back, Carmina said, "And this is María, my *madrina*. Did you meet her the other night?"

"No," Miguel answered, smiling at the graying, motherly-looking woman in her late fifties. "Pleased to meet you."

She nodded at him coolly. "So you're Miguel. I heard what you did." Her eyes narrowed. "That you stole the dove's head."

"María!" Carmina huffed. "We've already discussed that. It's not important now. It was an accident. Nothing happened. Please..."

"Nothing happened yet," the woman snapped, still staring coldly at Miguel.

Ileana stepped over and took his arm protectively, then glared at María. "*Basta*, señora, enough," she said dryly. "Come on, Miguel. Let's eat."

"I'm sorry," Carmina offered as they turned to leave. "Please understand that she's only concerned with my welfare. That's all. It's nothing to worry about."

Ileana smiled back at her. "I know," she said softly.

Miguel glanced around. Fortunately, no one seemed to have overheard the exchange. Still, he asked Ileana if they should go.

"No," she said emphatically. "We can't let her ruin the fun. That one's an old hen. You must forgive her ways."

"I need a drink," Miguel droned. "They serve liquor at these things?"

A couple of tall glasses of rum-and-coke later and Miguel felt better, much better in fact, and hungry. Ileana was already on her second helping, and from the gleeful way she was surveying the lavish spread of food, it was obvious she was going to have more. He'd read somewhere, *Playboy* maybe, that girls with hearty appetites made great lovers, and she'd done nothing to disprove that dictum.

Miguel stepped up to the table beside her. On large white platters were pork chunks, roasted chicken, whole baked fish wrapped in banana leaves, peeled shrimp, crab meat, spicy meat patties, conch fritters, hard-boiled eggs, dumplings, black beans and rice, okra, yucca, plantains, chiles, mangos, papayas, coconuts and lots of pastries and a few other things he couldn't identify. There were no utensils, however. Everyone was eating with their fingers. "It would be offensive to the *orishas*," Ileana had told him, "to use spoons and forks and especially knives."

He picked up a white plate and nodded at a steaming mound of meat. "What's that?"

She licked her lips. "Curried goat. It's one of my favorites."

"Sounds great," he said. "Think I'll try that, too, and have another drink."

While they were eating, Ileana introduced him to most of the people, including several blacks and a couple of Anglos. Most, however, were middle-aged, middle-class Cubans. Miguel recognized some of them from Carmina's initiation. They were a friendly group, flowing around and around the buffet, laughing merrily and clearly enjoying themselves. No one seemed to question his presence, although once out of the corner of his eye he had seen María conferring with Rosa and gesturing in his direction. That troubled him. The old *madrina* could cause problems between him and Rosa. Besides that, she had a look in her eyes that was frightening.

After an hour or so, most of the food had been consumed, and the women began picking up the plates and platters and putting them into boxes stowed under the tables. To Miguel's delight, since he felt he might need another drink or two before the evening was over, the liquor was left in place and a man was refilling the ice buckets from a large Coleman cooler. Soon candles were brought out and placed on the tables. Some were arranged in a sweeping half circle on the cement floor. It was interesting, Miguel noted, how once the candles were lit and the overhead lights turned off, the mood changed instantly. Everyone now spoke in hushed voices and began moving closer together, congregating finally on the floor between the half circle of flickering, smokey light.

"They should be here any minute," Ileana whispered as they sat down at the very back of the group.

"Who should be here?"

"The *batá* drummers."

No sooner had she said that when a side door opened and three solemn-faced black men walked in. They formed a single file, each with a different-size drum hanging from a leather cord slung over his shoulder. Without glancing even once at the assembly, they took their places behind the arc of candles and began to softly tap out the highly syncopated, primal rhythms. The effect was immediate and mesmerizing. The people began to sway.

Miguel tries to follow the rhythmic call and response. The drums are beckoning the saints, asking them to come down, to take over. Soon he loses concentration. Finally his eyes close and his body and mind give in to the hollow, hypnotic sounds. Images of African jungles overpower him, dissolve, recrystallize and then flicker away, only to form again. Dark and dank jungles. Forbidding yet peaceful jungles. Jungles with monkeys chattering in the forest canopy, pythons twisted around branches hanging over moss-covered paths, leopards lurking in the shadows, parrots with plumage so brilliant they seem to mock the world of green. Jungles where ferocious, luridly-painted purple-black faces peer through the dense foliage and then vanish. Jungles where heavy-breasted native women laugh and call from their beds on the soft forest floor. Jungles where wild-eyed shamen dance around elaborately carved wooden idols. Jungles littered with thousands of chained slaves screaming in agony to the incessant throbbing of drums, talking drums, laughing drums, crying drums, drums drums drums.

And finally they stop.

Miguel shakes his head and looks up as the three players step out the side door, the shortest one drags on a cigarette and puts on a pair of aviator sunglasses. He glances at his watch. They had played continuously for an hour and forty minutes.

"I feel like I've slept for days," Ileana yawns, patting her mouth. Miguel stands, he stretches. He too feels refreshed in spite of the time spent sitting on the cement floor. They go searching for drinks.

A rum-and-coke in hand, Ileana whispers in Miguel's ear. "I don't take *santería* too seriously. It's

just a game." She leans back and winks at him, sharing
her secret.

But he is confused by her confession, if it was a
confession. Is she saying that all of this was fun and
games for her, entertainment, something she is
involved in because of personal circumstances and not
out of heart-felt belief? He isn't sure. She has made
comments before about the cult that were ambivalent,
even contradictory. And what is most important: Does
it really matter to him how she feels about it all?

Again, Miguel is not sure. His feelings toward
Ileana have grown stronger over the past couple of
weeks. So has his apprehension over her active partici-
pation in the cult's rituals. Several times he has wanted
to ask her outright, but has avoided putting her on the
spot. Maybe he doesn't want to know, not yet. For now
he is happier than ever before. Why rush things? he
tells himself. When the time is right all of his questions
will be answered, then he can decide one way or another whether he cares about her enough to accept her
religious convictions, no matter how bizarre they
appear to be.

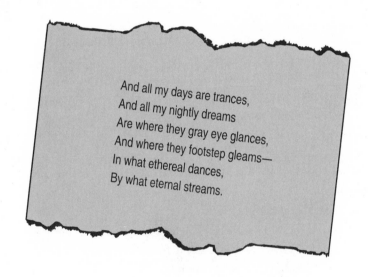

And all my days are trances,
And all my nightly dreams
Are where they gray eye glances,
And where they footstep gleams—
In what ethereal dances,
By what eternal streams.

Edgar Allan Poe, *To One in Paradise*

15
OH WHEN THE SAINTS

By the time they'd refreshed their drinks (Miguel's fifth of the evening) and had worked their way around to the back of the group, a woman was standing in a circle drawn with charcoal in the middle of the room. She chanted the same phrase over and over: *"Espíritu de santo, espíritu de santo..."* Within a few minutes she gave way to someone else, who in turn soon relinquished center circle to yet someone else. And so it went for an hour or more, everything very fluid and casual with the litany of countless repetitions being led by a variety of people who shifted back and forth between Latin and Spanish and English and even Yoruba. But all along the intensity was building until finally everyone, it seemed, was caught up in the spirit of the chants.

Suddenly, out of nowhere, as if they'd just materialized, the drums kicked in, louder and more urgent than before. A spontaneous cheer greeted them, and people began to clap and sway. It was perfect timing, Miguel thought, turning to watch the unsmiling *oloris* beating away. The shortest of the drummers, still wearing his dark aviator shades, was playing the *konkolo* drum.

Almost immediately a black man who went by the nickname of Chuey was drag-stepping into the circle, bobbing his shaved head to and fro and clapping on the off-beat. When the skinny little guy broke into a rumba, another cheer went up. Then, out of the crowd, danced Mercedes, the old gatekeeper, lifting her white robe just enough to clear her ankles, revealing a pair of tennis shoes on her feet. Everyone laughed and several of the men whistled cat-calls and yelled *"azúcar,"* sugar, as the old lady began to move her ancient hips, reaching out for Chuey who was playing his part perfectly, staring at her longingly as if she were the most beautiful woman ever to grace a dance floor. But soon they were engulfed by other dancers—some dancing solo, others as couples and still others in groups of three and four, holding hands and swinging both around and around and in and out.

Just then, as Miguel and Ileana were laughing and starting to embrace, Carmina's voice called from twenty feet away. "So there you love birds are. Come on, Ileana," she said, waving, "let's dance."

Standing at the liquor table, a fresh drink in hand, Miguel watches the girls samba-walk into the crowded circle. Nearly everyone is dancing now, really moving about and singing chants and clapping to the spellbinding rhythmic sounds which grow louder and louder, and faster and faster. The scene is almost pagan, he thought, the way the celebrants revel in the aura of primitive energy they created and which drives them on. Again he is struck by how African it all is, how tribal. The entire ceremony beginning with the meal, a communal feast, eaten without western utensils.

Abruptly the drumming stops, except for a slow, steady beat coming from the large *iya* drum. Within moments the circle is empty and everyone crowded around its perimeter, eyes fixed on the *batás*. At the back of the group, Miguel spots Ileana, motioning with her head for him to join her. He takes her hand, moist from dancing, and feels the collective excitement and sense of expectation. Conversations have stopped and it is quiet for the first time this evening. It is eerie, he thinks. The deep bass tone of the *iya* reverberates around the emptiness of the warehouse and sounds like the heartbeat of a giant.

Within seconds the *batás* break into a loud, liturgical-like cadence. Miguel shakes his head and inhales deeply. For an instant there, he is sure he feels, smells even, an ocean breeze, brisk and with a tang of salt. Then someone yells, "*Yemayá*, it's *Yemayá!*" But the smell of the sea vanishes. He detects only the odor of perspiration and the fragrance of cheap perfumes and scented candles.

He looks around. Everyone is pleased that the drums have announced the arrival of *Yemayá*, goddess of the sea. Then off to his left he hears a commotion. People stepping aside. They clear a path to the circle.

Staggering heavy-legged into it, shoulders slump, jaw dragging, eyes rolling, is Hernán.

"*Yemayá's* mounted Hernán!" "Look, it's Hernán she wanted!" he hears Ileana and the others cry.

Hernán is standing at attention in the middle of the circle, eyes bulging. He begins to quiver, then to shake violently from head to toe. Miguel chuckles as he watches the big man's belly, protruding from the bottom of the "Miami Vice" T-shirt, flop heavily up and down over the top of his pants. It really looks as if he is being possessed, his body if not his mind fights the invasion but cannot prevent it.

After two horrible jolts that nearly floor him, Hernán goes limp, meat hanging on the bones. His dazed eyes stare at a distant point. He remains that way for a while, hunched over, totally relaxed. You can see that life is returning to his eyes until finally they are clear. Soon they begin to sparkle, then to glow mischievously, amused as they scan people toeing the edge of the charcoal-lined circle and opened-mouth.

In a slow, snake-like motion Hernán straightens up, then throws his head back and laughs haughtily in a bewitchingly feminine voice that echoes around the warehouse and hangs in the rafters for an inordinate amount of time. Then he laughs again and again until the building booms with the disdainful laughter that drowns out the shouts of "*Yemayá!*" "*Yemayá!*"

With a leap Yemayá takes off, running straight-legged and high on her toes in a *pas de bourée* around and around the circle, winking and blowing limp-wristed kisses to a chorus of howling admirers. They call and plead for her attention and extend offerings of candy and drinks. They wave twenty, fifty, and hundred-dollar bills before the saint's eyes.

Miguel stands there, stunned by the metamorphosis which has occurred in Hernán. But the change is not very tangible. Except for the way Hernán's new voice projects and hangs in the air and his eyes glow with a piercing light so distant it seems astral, he is physically the same. Still it cannot be denied that a profound change has taken place. An ethereal presence, immediate, powerful, surrounds Hernán. It alters the act of perception itself.

Yemayá is now teasing her audience, stopping here and there to accept an offering. Then she backs away laughing, then vamping and cooing, sweat streaming down her face.

Fanning herself, she steps up close to the man. "What do you wish of *Yemayá?*"

The man staggers around a bit, looking more than a little intoxicated. He tries to sound formal but slurs his words. "If it pleases the great *Yemayá*, I desire only to step into your kingdom."

"Then you shall," she mocks, "you shall. Come with me to the sea. Come swim with *Yemayá.*"

To cheers and applause they swim across the circle a couple of times, the man backstroking and having the time of his life, until *Yemayá* splashes him out of the water and he stumbles into the crowd.

Yemayá/Hernán stands joyful and triumphant, surveying the group. "*Yemayá* feels like dancing. Who would like to dance with *Yemayá?*" she asks.

Arms shoot up, waving frantically, trying to catch her roving eyes. "I would!" people scream. "Here, *Yemayá*, here!"

Again she teases them, asking with a whimper, "Wouldn't *anyone* like to dance with *Yemayá?*"

The place roars and *Yemayá's* laughter bounces off the walls. "Okay, okay, since you love *Yemayá* so much, I will lead you all in a conga dance. Come," she beckons.

"Oh, boy," Ileana shouts, "a conga line! Let's go, Miguel!"

He resists her pull. She remembers Rosa's warning not to get involved.

"But we have to. No one should disappoint an *orisha*. Rosa knows that. And besides," Ileana shrugs, "you can't believe everything Rosa says, take my word for it."

The line has formed quickly, *Yemayá* in the lead, of course, and Carmina at the rear, looking over her shoulder and laughing and wiggling her boyish hips invitingly. Miguel shrugs, grabs on to her waist, Ileana behind him, tickling his sides, and off they go, this way and that way, zigging and zagging, in and out of the circle in great swooping figure-eights.

Miguel is soon sweating. He can feel himself growing light-headed from the liquor, but decides it is okay. What the hell? he thinks. It feels good to relax again, even if he had to bat his eyes occasionally to keep from seeing double. And, as the line moves faster and faster to the relentless, increasing tempo of the drums, he makes a discovery. Hidden within the complex of rhythms is a very, very subtle melody. Finally, as people began to stumble, exhausted, the line breaks down, and *Yemayá* hustles everyone out of the circle.

Standing there panting, drenched with sweat, *Yemayá* lifts up the T-shirt to mop her face. And when she does, another cheer goes up as the tattoo is unveiled. Looking down her nose at it, *Yemayá* grins, tucks the T-shirt under her chin and begins to roll her belly, causing the tattoo to undulate lewdly as people hoot and cat-call.

By now the drumming has become wilder, more reckless, deafening. Arms held straight out from her sides, *Yemayá* starts slowly to spin in place and then builds up speed, going faster and faster. She then begins to whirl clumsily about the circle until finally she loses her balance completely and collapses in a heap on the floor.

Foam issues from her twitching mouth.

Miguel feels suddenly drained. He feels sick at his stomach when he stares at Hernán, lying there like a beached whale, his face lifeless and blanched. He glances around, but no one else seems disturbed by the

sight, not even Ileana who like the others is listening
intently to the deep, solitary beat of the *iya*, signaling
that yet another *orisha* is being summoned.

As they spin out of the parking lot, Ileana at the wheel,
Miguel can still hear the drums and feel the inferno-like heat
of the warehouse. He rolls down the window and breathes
deeply, grateful that it is late fall and the air is cool. His head
is spinning and he wishes he hadn't drunk so much.

Although María was possessed by *Shangó* only minutes
ago, already it is like a dream, hazy and difficult to recall in
its entirety, but with flashes of clarity.

He remembers now that when *Shangó's* cadence began,
there had been a rush of hot air that blew out all but a hand-
ful of candles, leaving the place in near-darkness. Those who
were smoking quickly extinguished their cigarettes and cigars. They were deferring to *Shangó*, owner of fire and god of
thunder and lightning. Ileana is excited. But then it is María,
Carmina's *madrina*, who stalks into the circle fully possessed,
pointing a finger at Hernán and bellowing angrily about "that
thing" *Yemayá* dared leave behind. Her excitement turned to
concern; you could see it in her face.

Ileana reached for Miguel's arm and nodded toward the
door.

They backed away from the rapt crowd, still watching
María who now stood over Hernán, taunting his slumped
mass unmercifully. There was movement on the far side of the
room which caught Miguel's eye.

Pacing back and forth impatiently, a red cape draped over
her shoulders, was Rosa.

Shouts of "*Shangó!*" "*Shangó!*" rang out.

In the circle, María was holding Hernán in the air as if he
were no more than a rag doll.

They turned and sprinted for the door. Ileana out, Miguel looked back. María was laughing demonically and pointing to Rosa who stood there calmly, her hand posed unflinchingly in the flames of a large candle.

"I saw the *mal ojo*, the evil eye," Ileana says. "I saw it right away, as soon as María walked in the circle. That's how it is with *Shangó*...you never can tell how he'll be. But I didn't like that evil eye. Did you see it, Miguel? Miguel?"

He was fast asleep.

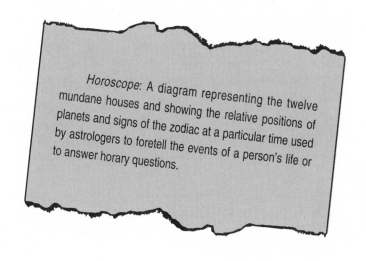

Horoscope: A diagram representing the twelve mundane houses and showing the relative positions of planets and signs of the zodiac at a particular time used by astrologers to foretell the events of a person's life or to answer horary questions.

Webster's Third New International Dictionary

16

OUT WITH THE OLD, IN WITH THE NEW

"It's no use," Vicki said.

By the tone of her voice, Miguel wasn't sure if her feelings were hurt or if she was just disgusted that he couldn't perform. Probably both, he decided.

She rolled off him and reached for her new nightgown, one of those short-short baby-doll numbers called "Naughty Angel" by Frederick's of Hollywood. "I knew it was over," she mumbled more to herself than to him as she slipped on the sheer white silk nightie with peek-a-boo nipple holes. "I just knew it." Now her voice became sing-songy and she moved her head from side to side. "First you say you're too busy to see me. Then you stop calling. And now...now you can't even make love to me."

Miguel was pissed he'd put himself into this position. For at least the tenth time in the last hour he wondered why he hadn't ended it on the phone this morning when she'd called. That would have been less embarrassing for both of them. He still could have cleared the air, said there were no hard feelings, that it just hadn't worked out, that's all, and have wished her well. Sure there were a few things of his he wanted to pick up—some clothes, a few books, a couple of CDs. But he could have picked 'em up later or just have written 'em off. So there must have been another reason why he'd told her he wanted to see her, although when she'd called, he didn't know (or at least hadn't admitted it to himself) what it was.

Now he knew. It was a test to see Vicki again, to measure not so much how he felt about her, but about Ileana. And the answer was clear. From the very moment Vicki opened the door, he was sorry he'd come over. But there she stood in that baby-doll nightie looking so outrageously sexy she seemed more like a glossy caricature of feminine sexual attraction than a real woman.

Before he could even say "hi," her hand went to his mouth. "Sssh, we can talk later," she'd whispered, pulling him toward the bedroom, backing up on her tip-toes, giving him her best moist-lip tigress look. He remembered thinking at the time that he should level with her right then and there, get it over with, but then asking himself what difference would it make if they got it on one last time.

Yet, even as good as she looked and tight and willing as she felt, the pangs of guilt grew stronger by the moment until finally he realized that this macho behavior just wasn't his style, that his life had changed since he'd become involved in this *santería* assignment. Thinking about that, and just before Vicki gave up and pushed him off, he realized he hadn't attended a single football game this fall.

"It's that girl at the *botánica*, isn't it?" Vicki said. "Okay, don't say anything, but I still know it is."

She was leaning against the headboard, arms crossed covering the peek-a-boo holes. "I've heard that's how you Cuban guys are…"

He was sitting on the edge of the bed buttoning his shirt. Without looking up, he said, "Meaning?…"

She stared patronizingly at his back. "Meaning that American girls are okay for sex and show, but not to marry, right?"

He smiled to himself, acknowledging there was a grain of truth in her assertion, although he'd never really thought about it when it came to the two of them. But, yeah, maybe that was it all along—sex and show. He said, "Did I ever once mention marriage?"

"It's not important now," she snapped. "It's over!"

Vicki scrambled off the bed. She put on a fluffy white terry-cloth bathrobe and started pacing back and forth on the side of the bed opposite Miguel.

"You know," she said thoughtfully, "it's like *totally unreal* how I knew it was over this morning when I read our horoscopes. That's why I called. I didn't want to believe it. And when you said you had to see me, I thought, well, maybe there was still hope for us. And so I went out shopping to find something special... Oh, that's not important now. It's just *totally unreal* how I knew it was over. Know what our horoscopes said?" She saw his shoulders shrug. "Mine said, 'Find out where you stand. It's time to make a decision.' Yours said, 'Out with the old, in with the new.'"

Vicki stopped pacing. "Don't laugh at me," she whimpered. "You think you're so cool, but you don't know how dumb you are...falling for some freaky voodoo girl who dresses like, like Carmen Miranda."

Miguel stood and faced her. "Listen, Vicki, I'm sorry about everything—tonight, the last few weeks, everything. It's just that, I don't know. Either we're not, or I'm not..."

"Oh, please," she groaned, "spare me the excuses, you two-timing turd."

Miguel wanted to go to Ileana's, but he just couldn't bring himself to head straight over there—not with the feel of Vicki's body still fresh on his fingertips, the air around him redolent with the flowery fragrance of Vicki's hibiscus perfume. Even a two-timing turd has some principles, he thought derisively.

Just ahead was the intersection of North Kendall Drive and Dixie Highway. He considered his options. If it were afternoon instead of early evening, he'd probably turn right on Dixie and cruise on down south to Key Largo. He would stop in at Alabama Jack's or The Caribbean Club and have a few beers and watch the sunset over Florida Bay. Of course, two of his favorite malls to stroll and people-watch, Dadeland and The Falls, weren't far away. But he just wasn't in the mood tonight for hassling with throngs of consumption-addicted shoppers.

He turned north on Dixie and immediately spotted the Tony Roma's sign and realized he was hungry, although he wasn't up for their speciality of baby-back ribs and loaves of onion rings. Passing Sunset Avenue, he considered going to Monty's at the marina in the Grove where he could listen to reggae and munch on conch fritters. Or maybe he'd swing over to Miami Beach and catch some jazz or blues and mingle with the oh-so-hip pretty people in the art-deco district. He considered other possibilities only to dismiss them as fast as he thought of 'em, literally shaking his head as he drove.

At Red Road he abruptly hung a left and shortly pulled into the dirt parking lot of Bill and Ted's. It was a nondescript tavern located by the railroad tracks across the street from the university in a seedy strip of warehouses and repair shops that bordered South Miami's ghetto. The owners were a couple of old guys who'd bought the place when they got out of the Navy. They made sure that, in spite of the location and outward appearance, their tavern was a clean and friendly place to drink beer. Besides, they had the best burgers in town, served plain or "all the way" with cheese and grilled onions but never with any "salad." Salad, by the way, was what Bill and Ted called the lettuce and tomato misguided people put on burgers.

He ordered a Bud and a burger "all the way," and as he ate, he thought of Ileana and how little they'd done in the four weeks they'd been together. Not once, he now realized, had they gone out to dinner or taken in a movie or, for that matter, even mentioned anything about going out. All their time, virtually every night since Carmina's initiation, had been spent at Ileana's place, except for the drum ceremony they'd attended a week before.

Most evenings Miguel would arrive around nine, and for the next three or four hours they might listen to those old Latin dance tunes, drink a little rum, maybe read aloud a poem or two by José Martí or some other Cuban poet, and occasionally fix a late meal. But mainly they spent their time in bed, just holding each other, making love and talking.

During those heady, suspended hours in bed or on the floor of her cushion-filled living room, their conversation would invariably turn to Cuba. Strangely, it now seemed to him, they spoke only of dreamy remembrances about their childhoods on the island, the things they used to do, their families. Increasingly they talked in Spanish, and for the first time in as long as he could remember, Miguel was beginning to actually think, and even dream, in Spanish. Perhaps it was their way of avoiding any subject that might dampen their thrill in being together. Whatever the reason, not once had either Miguel or Ileana discussed their present situations or made plans for the future.

So while he had learned a lot about her youth—that her parents had died in a fire when she was an infant, that she had been raised by her aunt, and that her aunt was practically a *santera*—in truth Miguel knew no more about Ileana by now than after their first night together.

By the same token, Ileana knew little of Miguel's present life, only that he was a graduate student working on a research assignment on *santería*. She hadn't asked why or how he'd become interested in the cult. He, in turn, had not mentioned to Ileana that the story he'd read in the newspaper about the stolen skull and the subsequent murder were the catalysts for his interest in the cult. In fact, prior to the drum ceremony their conversation regarding *santería* had been of a superficial nature at best. The ceremony had troubled them both, he realized. Yet as much as Miguel wanted to get things out in the open, he expected Ileana to break the ice.

But maybe she had been trying all along, it now occurred to Miguel. Only two nights before when they were talking about Cuba and looking at old photographs, she had said out of the blue, "On the island, people call upon the *orishas* to bring joy and harmony to their lives. They were so much fun there." Why hadn't he followed up on that? And earlier in the week she had mentioned that she'd not gone to the *botánica* for several days, that it would it be nice to live and work in a place where there wasn't "a constant shadow over you." But that comment had sounded so cryptic that Miguel hadn't given it much thought at the time. Now, in retrospect, it seemed obvious to Miguel that Ileana had been trying to bring the discussion of *santería* out in the open.

"Wanna another sandwich?"

Miguel looked up and smiled at Ted. He was the only guy he knew who called a hamburger a sandwich.

Lying on the floor, her head resting comfortably on a soft pillow, Ileana stares at the ceiling fan, enjoying its steady rhythm as much as its cooling effects. Her mind spins around and around with the blades until finally she closes her eyes and drifts. Yes, my life was sheltered. I see that now. But Tía had insisted. And who could have resisted her? My only relative. A *santera*! Didn't she pay for my private tutors? Didn't she buy me the best? Okay, I was lonely. I admit that now. But, oh, our *santería* friends—Juan, Gloria, Humberto, Sylvia—were such good friends. Then she had to die, my Tía, my sweet Tía. What was I to do? Without her? The house so big. The gardens. And then, I have to admit this. I wanted something else, something new, a change. She had spoken of Rosa, my mother's best friend. She lived in Miami. Miami! MIAMI! I wrote her. Rosa said, "Come, my child, a new life awaits."

I was content enough at first, working in the *botánica*, meeting Rosa and Hernán's clients. But Rosa had insisted that I should think only of the *orishas*. That I keep myself clean for them. "Live only for their glory!" she kept repeating. Rosa wouldn't let me meet anyone, not anyone unless they were clients or *santeros*. What had I gained by coming to Miami? My life was worse than in Cuba. My Tía wasn't here. I had no friends. And Rosa's constant obsession with her masters! Never could we do enough to please them. I wanted to run away. Go anywhere. But Rosa would have found me. No matter where I went. I knew that. I was so alone. So confused.

Then Hernán bought his new house. He said I could have the *casita* in back. My own little house! Never had I lived in a house of my own. It was fun, fixing it up. Doing as I pleased. Away from Rosa. And her masters. I felt happy for the first time in this country. I felt...free.

But Rosa said that I had betrayed her—and the *orishas*— by moving out. She wouldn't even talk to me for the longest time. Then when I saw her next. She was different. Sweet, sometimes. But detached, far away. You could see it in her eyes. All she would talk about was purifying *santería*. She said everybody was corrupting the faith. Weakening its vitality. That the only way to recapture its strength, its truth, was to return to the ancient practices. It was like Rosa was on a mission, a crusade.

Far worse, at all the ceremonies—and at other times, too, without even making the saint!—Rosa would be possessed by *Shangó*. You could count on it. And when he mounted her, *Shangó* always played with fire. Never his other weapons. Only fire. Fire, fire, fire! How I hate it! The way it took away my mother and father. Leaving me...

Standing on Ileana's front porch, Miguel remembered the grilled onions and the burger and huffed in his hands to test the smell of his breath. Better have a couple of those mint sprigs, he decided. Once he'd asked her why she ate mint and she'd replied, "Because it makes your breath smell good." Okay, so no mystery there.

He knocked on the door.

Later, lying in bed, their arms around each other, Miguel said, "And another thing, how'd you like to go to a Dolphin game?"

She paused and then asked, "What kind of games do dolphins play?"

He laughed. "I'll be right back. That'll take some explaining."

In the bathroom he opened up the cabinet to get a towel. And of course...he spotted the jar with the photos, the panties and the bloody tissue.

In anthropology we distinguish among several forms of magic. There's white magic, which is used for good or protective purposes. Most folk religions, including *santería*, practice only white magic. Of course, its antithesis is black magic, which deals in revenge and ill-fortune. For example, the followers of *vodun*, or "voodoo" as most people call it, incorporate black magic into their belief system. Then there's sympathetic magic. It operates under the premise that one thing or event can affect another at a distance because of a sympathetic connection between them. It's divided into two branches, including imitative or homeopathic magic which attempts to control fate through the mimicking of a desired event. Undoubtedly, you've heard of people sticking pins in dolls as a means of injuring or even killing someone. That, of course, is a form of homeopathic magic.

From Miguel Calderón's recorded lectures notes of October II, Prof. Krajewski's ethnology class.

17
THAT OLD WHITE MAGIC

"The *amarre* is an example, a rather enchanting example I'd like to think, of contagious magic," Professor Krajewski was explaining to Miguel. "It's predicated on the notion that things once in contact with a person remain so permanently, regardless of how separated physically they become. It can also be used to work magic against them."

Miguel nodded understandingly. "So my semen and blood and her panties tied us together and supposedly prevented me from getting an erection with someone other than Ileana."

The professor blinked an affirmative.

"And the photos?"

"Well," the professor said slowly, "I think their inclusion was more romantic than ritualistic. An *amarre*, a love potion if you will, is a most enchanting form of contagious magic. Quite harmless, really."

"So it's basically just a lot of hocus-pocus."

The professor furrowed his brow. "Now, we shouldn't be too quick to dismiss these forms of magic as merely hocus-pocus, should we."

Remembering his limp effort at Vicki's, which he did not feel any need to relate to Krajewski, Miguel had to agree. "I see your point. I guess it was presumptuous of me to assume that. After all, there could be something to it, right?"

The professor smiled in a noncommittal way. "What we as anthropologists should know better than most is that all cultures, including our own, have their superstitions and phobias."

"You mean, like not walking under a ladder, avoiding cracks in sidewalks or throwing salt over the shoulder. That kind of superstition?"

"Yes, that's right. And think of all the signs for fortune tellers and palm readers you've seen around this town. And then there's the astrology charts in the newspapers."

Miguel thought of Vicki. ("Out with the old, in with the new.")

"And of course," the professor went on, "there's trikaidekaphobia."

"What?"

"Trikaidekaphobia, fear of number thirteenth."

"Friday the thirteen! for example."

The professor nodded. "You'd be surprised at the number of skyscrapers that don't have a thirteenth floor, and airplanes without a thirteenth aisle."

"Okay, in other words we have to respect these various forms of magic and superstition regardless of how irrational or illogical they may seem."

The professor relit his pipe. "Respect for value systems is certainly part of it, but we have to bear in mind as well that concepts of rationality and logic vary from culture to culture."

Miguel said, "Are you saying these things work or don't work?"

"What I'm suggesting is that it's all a matter of perception, both for the participant and the observer. Think of what you witnessed at the *santos subidos*, the possession ceremony. Were those feats that astounded you real, or did they only seem real?"

"Believe me, I've been wondering about that," Miguel exclaimed.

"Well then, let's reconsider what happened. The first phase of the ceremony, as you correctly observed, set the stage for the sacred theatrics that followed by fostering a sense of communality which put the celebrants in an open, receptive frame of mind."

"And it was so African," Miguel chimed in.

"Yes, African in tandem with the experience of slavery. You see, rituals like this, where everyone is actively leading chants, singing and dancing, evolved in part out of the slave mentality. For a while, during the ceremony at least, a slave could feel he was somebody, not merely an object, a commodity."

"Even a god," Miguel offered.

The professor looked at him gravely. "Yes, even a god."

"But what about the things that happened later, the 'sacred theatrics' you called 'em?"

The professor put down his pipe and leaned back in his chair. He coughed a couple of times, hitting his frail chest with his fist as he did. "First of all, what you probably weren't aware of at the time is that, in addition to creating a kind of tribal bonding, the initial phase of the ceremony—the chanting, the *batá* music, the liquor, the use of candles, even the late hour—contributed to an altered state of perception. Beyond that, much of what you saw is an issue of mind over matter."

"So, for example," Miguel asked skeptically, "I only *thought* I heard Hernán's *Yemayá* voice sound like it was coming from a loudspeaker?"

"In part your condition contributed to that perception, yes. But it also was a function of acoustics; sounds can easily be distorted in a large empty structure. And, for his part, if Hernán felt the persona of *Yemayá* called for such a voice, then he would attempt to project it in a superhuman fashion, perhaps with success. Your perception, then, was the result of a combination of these factors."

Miguel shook his head in a resigned manner. "I still find it hard to believe that María, who weighs no more than 140 and is probably 50 or 60 years old, could lift a man like Hernán. Besides Hernán's 300 or more pounds were dead weight at the time. He was totally limp."

"I recognize it appears improbable, but we mustn't forget that biochemical changes were taking place. She undoubtedly was operating with a tremendous boost of adrenaline. Remember, the body is an untapped reservoir of strength. You've surely heard the stories of this reservoir being unleashed during periods of flight and fright. The mother who lifts a car to save her trapped child."

"But this wasn't a period of flight or fright."

"Oh?" Professor Krajewski said wryly. "The style of the *orishas*, Miguel, is authoritarian. Much of their public behavior takes the form of psychic aggression, which is one explanation for their almost predictably capricious actions. It's all a way of gaining control. And why? Because the world itself is frightening, and one needs all the help one can muster, including for some, aggressive yet sympathetic deities. It's a question of survival."

"So when Rosa held her hand in the flame of the candle it was a form of psychic aggression. But against who was that aggression directed?" Miguel asked. "Me?"

"You, and the rest of the world for that matter."

"Okay, let's say that's why she did it, but again: How? Her hand didn't move an inch and she had this weird look on her face as if she really enjoyed being burned. That was the scariest part."

"Look, Miguel, I'm not saying it didn't happen. It's just that...well...the same as the mystics in India who lie on a bed of nails: It's true, yes, but there's also technique involved. For all we know she could have dipped her hand in a pyroretardant liquid before sticking it in the flame."

Miguel laughed out loud. "You mean, someone would actually do something like that?"

"It's not beyond them," the professor said matter-of-factly. "In truth, we must appreciate that there's a certain amount of theater involved in all this. It could almost be considered an operatic art form, I've often thought."

Miguel tried to think of Hernán's comical-grotesque performance as *Yemayá* in operatic terms. "I see what you mean." He smiled. "But I imagine Verdi would roll over in his grave." He paused. "By the way, what's the significance of the circle?"

"The circle and the conga line, among other nonlinear features of the ceremony, are precautionary measures against the encroachment of evil. Evil, you see, moves only in straight lines."

Krajewski leans back in his chair. Guess I should go ahead and ask him, get it over with, the professor thought, sitting up in his chair very casually. "And how old did you say she was, Ileana I mean?"

He watched Miguel shrug his shoulders and smile sheepishly. "Gee, I've never bothered to ask."

Can you believe it? He never asked! "Come now, lad, surely you've inquired as to her age."

"I don't know why I didn't, exactly. It's just that our relationship..."

Look, his face is flushed. I've embarrassed him. So he is embarrassed! I must persist! "Can you venture a guess?"

"Around my age, I think."

Well, if he thinks she might be *around* his age, then the possibility exists. My God, it could be true! "Experience has taught me that men tend to greatly underestimate the age of women. And that's probably for the best, Calderón, that's probably for the best."

Perhaps I should instruct the lad to ask Ileana directly. No, I think he got the message. I mustn't appear too anxious. Stay calm about this. Stay calm. I'll know soon enough. "Well, I have a lecture scheduled in two minutes, Calderón. But we can discuss this matter latter, can't we."

Its nearly midnight. Maybe she's already in bed. I could call another time. No, do it now! Get on with it! Just one more sip of this gin-and-tonic. Okay, dial the number. "Hello, Rosa. This is Henry. We must talk."

Murder will out.

Cervantes, *Don Quixote*

18
KEEP 'EM CLOSED

Hernán spoke in Spanish, his tone exaggeratedly ecclesiastical. "According to the dictates of the ancient and omnipotent *orishas*, and by the sacred powers vested in me as a *babalao*, I serve notice to the world that you..." He glanced over at Rosa.

"Xavier," she whispered.

He nodded. "That you, Xavier, for now and forever, by virtue of your most generous offering to the *orishas*, have been initiated as one of their siblings, as a brother, with all the rights and privileges pertaining thereto."

As Hernán turned solemnly toward the blood-splattered altar, he winked at Dago, who'd maintained this same bemused smirk on his ebony face since the ceremony had begun.

Candy was ecstatic. Joyfully hugging Rosa, he kept saying *"fantástico"* over and over. Although he had yet to screw her, he already thought he could feel the *aché*, the power, and he silently thanked Enrique, his old cellmate. Damn if the old fag hadn't been right. *"Fantástico!"*

By this time Hernán and Dago had already picked up a few things and were heading out the door of the shed, Dago carefully wiping the blade of his short machete with a soft oiled cloth.

"Come on," Rosa urged, tugging on Candy's arm. "We've got to hurry."

Oh, she's excited now, Candy thought, smiling cockily to himself. She's probably been dying for it all along; couldn't wait for the Candyman to slip it to her. Again he wondered what she was wearing under that *bruja* robe. Not that it made any difference at this point: He was ready for it. And after all, it only took one time; that's what his wise old storyteller buddy Enrique had said.

Rosa held the door open. The rush of night air off the river, although actually warm and humid, felt like a cool and fresh winter's breeze after the heat and heavy odor of death and decay inside. Tentatively, Candy glanced back at the macabre scene, and in his mind's eye could still see it all. That *negrito* slitting the goat's throat as he held its head back; the deep-red blood gushing out into an arch across the floor, drenching the fruit and the flowers; the decapitated chickens; the shiny skull. Damn, was he glad to get the fuck out of there.

Rosa said, pointing with her gloved hand across the vacant lot toward the darkened street, "We're going to take my car. It's the one behind Hernán's. You can wait there. I'll just be a minute, Xavier. Then we can be by ourselves."

There was no doubt about it now, that she was starving for it, Candy decided. Rosa's eyes were burning as they roamed up and down his body; her mouth was wet as she lingered on the phrase "by ourselves." Yeah, this was going to be even better than he had hoped. Feeling suddenly charitable, he thought he might even screw her twice, maybe once up the ass. Now, after prison, that had become his favorite way. "*Fantástico*," he said out loud.

Rosa opened the back door of the Plymouth as Dago was saying to Hernán, mockingly, "All the rights and privileges pertaining thereto? Wha' the fock?"

The two of them burst into a belly laugh that caused the car to shake. They looked back at Rosa. She had closed the door and was sitting in the middle of the back seat, the leather valise across her lap. She wasn't laughing, and her eyes had a glazed, liquid quality to them.

The giant and the dwarf looked at each other, then back at Rosa.

She'd unsnapped the latches and had flipped up the top. Dago, his chin resting on the back of the front seat, grinned back at her and said, "So, now he want to fock you, righ'?"

"*Fantástico*," Hernán chimed in.

Once again the car was shaking with their laughter.

Not bothering to look up from the valise where she was counting out bills, placing them in two neat stacks, a remote half-smile on her taunt round face, Rosa murmured, "Yes, and I might just let him. Whatever *Shangó* commands."

"Oh, I see," Dago said derisively. "And did *Shangó* command you to fock those other ones, too?"

Hernán was now laughing so hard he started hiccuping. This made Dago laugh all that much louder. Their laughter kept them from hearing Rosa say that *Shangó* had dealt with the others as he saw fit.

"Well," Rosa said as she closed and latched the leather case and slapped the two stacks of bills against the back of the front seat. "Here's your share—$15,000 each."

At the sight of the money the laughter stopped, that is until Hernán hiccuped and Dago said to Rosa, "Tha' extra five thousand is for you, jus' in case *Shangó* say, 'Go ahead and fock him?'"

From nearly a block away, as Rosa stood watching the Plymouth round the corner, she could still hear the hoots and howls. Valise in hand, she walked over to her car, a new red Oldsmobile Cutlass with a white top, opened the door and threw the case on the back seat. She crawled in front behind the wheel. Seductively, she smiled at Candy and motioned for him to scoot over next to her. When he did, she pulled the robe above her knees and took his hand. She put it underneath her garment and spread her legs. "I've been a long time without a man, Candy."

Now Candy knew. She wasn't wearing anything under that robe! And he couldn't believe how smooth and firm her legs were, what big and soft *chi-chis* she had. Breathing heavi-

ly now and nearly beside himself with glee and lust, Candy's
hand dropped back down to her undulating crotch.

Her head thrown back and her eyes closed, Rosa reached
for Candy's exploring hand. "No, not yet," she moaned, but
allowed a finger to probe a little deeper before gently pulling
his hand out from under the robe.

Rosa turned her head as Candy awkwardly tried to kiss
her. "Come on," he groaned, "we can do it right here. There's
enough room."

"If you like," she said, grabbing his hand as it shot back
under the garment. "It's just that...I forgot something, something important. We'll have to make a short trip and come
back to this place for a few minutes, no longer. Then, if you
like, we can do it here. Yes, there's enough room, there's plenty of room."

Driving back from the cemetery, the bag of dirt Rosa had
scraped up sitting on the floor of the front seat, Candy figured
he must have imagined it. That was the only possible explanation for how her *chi-chis*, which she'd allowed him to rub and
squeeze on the way back from the graveyard, had suddenly
turned as hard as stone. For an instant he considered reaching over and grabbing one just to make sure. But then,
remembering how incredibly strong her grip had been when
she'd yanked his hand away, he decided against it. Balefully,
out of the corners of his eyes, he looked over at her.

As if nothing had happened, she smiled at him excitedly
and said in a panting, husky voice, "We're almost there. Don't
worry, be patient. It'll be worth it." With a toss of her head she
blew him a kiss, and then, snake-like, rapidly flicked her
tongue at him.

Must've imagined it, he thought, getting hotter by the second as he watched her now sucking her middle finger, moving

it back and forth between her puckered lips. What else could
it be?

Walking carefully across the debris-littered lot, Candy
stared suspiciously at the little tin-top building by the river's
edge. Behind him Rosa was firmly, deeply massaging his ass
and whispering, "It'll only take a minute, no more. Then we'll
go back to the car. There's enough room, plenty of room."

Inside the shed Candy began to sweat at once. He
watched intently as Rosa placed the skull on the carcass of the
goat, already getting stiff, then sprinkle some of the cemetery
dirt on it before broadcasting handfuls about the room, on the
chickens and the flowers and the fruit and even on the ax with
the red and white tape on the handle that was leaning against
the wall.

Standing in front of him now, toying with one of the buttons on his shirt, Rosa said, "See, I told you it wouldn't take
long. We can go now if you like. But..." Slowly she started
unbuttoning his shirt. "Can't I feel you first? I can't wait to
feel you. Just relax, Xavier, relax..."

What the fuck? Candy thought, his shirt on the floor and
her hands now moving up and down his chest and stomach,
pinching his nipples, sending chills up his spine. If only he
knew for sure about her *chi-chis*, then everything would be
fine. Yes, he had to find out. It was the only way.

In a lunge, he grabbed for her.

But Rosa had dropped to her knees and was unzipping his
pants. In a second she had it out, hard and glistening. Instantly her mouth descended on the tip, then withdrew and she
blew on it softly.

Candy's knees buckled and he let out a guttural moan, his
hands reaching for her hair to pull her closer.

"Keep your eyes closed," Rosa said gravely. "Keep 'em closed. Keep 'em closed."

Candy wanted it so bad he ached. He wouldn't last long, he knew that much. Already he could feel it throbbing, ready to explode. But why had she stopped. Why had she...

Dear friend, all theory is gray,
And green the golden tree of life.

Goethe, *Mephistopheles and the Student.*

19
THE TWO ILEANAS

He knew it was coming.

All evening he'd been expecting the call, waiting there in the dimly-lighted living room in his favorite leather chair, legs outstretched on an ottoman, listening to classical music and sipping on a Jack Daniels and staring at the phone. When it hadn't come by 2 a.m., he decided he'd better get some sleep.

But his sleep was haunted. He dreamed he was skin diving and a monstrous eel, greenish-black in color with a thick serpent body, had bitten into his left bicep and was ripping and gnawing at it ferociously. If only he could move his free arm he might be able to distract it or even pry it off. But as hard as he tried, the arm just wouldn't respond. Suddenly, as he was on the verge of drowning, frantic and helpless in his immobility, the eel shot for his face.

And that's when the phone rang, at 5:46. A dull numbness throbbed up and down his cold, paralyzed arm and he realized it was asleep. Sitting on the edge of the bed, rubbing the arm and twitching his fingers to get the blood circulating, feeling it beginning to tingle finally, he counted nine rings before picking up the receiver.

"Gutiérrez," he said. Then shortly, "No, it isn't necessary, I know where it's at. I'm only a few blocks away. Yes, in Little Havana."

At 6 o'clock, already fully dressed, the Smith & Wesson in its plainclothes holster, he walked over to the night stand next to his bed, flipped open the address book, picked up the phone, and pushed the touch-tone buttons.

"Professor Krajewski? This is Lieutenant Gutiérrez, Miami P.D. I hate to disturb you at this hour, but it's urgent that I see you this morning. Would 8:30 at your office be convenient? Fine, and by the way, Professor, it's imperative that Miguel Calderón be there as well. Yes, your student. Would you call and ask that he join us? Well...I can't explain in detail on the phone, but I'm afraid we have another stolen skull."

The professor said, "So according to your theory we can expect a murder in two weeks."

Gutiérrez closed his eyes and nodded slightly.

Miguel glanced up at the calendar on the wall behind the professor's desk. "Two weeks from today will be December 5th, my birthday." He grinned sheepishly.

Gutiérrez smiled at him warmly. "Actually, I'm assuming the skull was disinterred yesterday, probably before midnight."

Interrupting, the professor said, "What cemetery did you say it was?"

"Woodlawn Memorial, on *Calle Ocho*. It was discovered this morning about daybreak when the caretaker was making his rounds."

Miguel said, "So it'll be December 4th...when the murder occurs, I mean."

Gutiérrez nodded. "Yes, the 4th." He paused. "On *Shangó's* feast day."

"Oh, shit!" Miguel groaned.

Gutiérrez turned to gaze plaintively out the sun-drenched window of the professor's office.

Miguel stared admiringly at the lieutenant, dressed this morning in an impeccable dark blue suit with a white silk shirt and a thin burgundy tie. You'd never guess that he was a cop, he kept thinking, not by the clothes he wore or by the way he spoke. Yet there was something about his eyes, penetrating and inalterably sad, that betrayed the reserved dignity and gentleness of his demeanor. Although he'd just met this aging, sartorially-improbable police lieutenant, he felt as if he'd known him forever and knew intuitively that he could trust him completely, even with his life if necessary.

Meanwhile, the professor had picked a big, drooping Sherlock Holmes, stared at his watch a moment, then reluctantly placed the pipe back in the round wooden holder. "I can appreciate now," he said to the lieutenant, eyes lingering on the pipe, "how you figured out the date when another skull would be stolen. Yet surely you had more substantive reasons for suspecting that one would be stolen."

Gutiérrez stood and straightened his suit. "For several weeks now," he began, "I've been monitoring the activities of three people whom we believe are suspects in the *santería* skull murders, as we've labeled them in the Department. One, Dagoberto, or simply 'Dago,' Villalobos, lives in Union City, New Jersey. It's unlikely either of you have met him, although we know he makes periodic trips to south Florida. The other two, however, live here and are known to both of you—Hernán Guerrero and Rosa García-Mesa."

Instantly Miguel thought of Ileana. No matter what, he had to get her out of there, away from those two. They could get their own apartment. He'd saved some money, enough anyway to cover a security deposit and first and last month's rent. And he could get a part-time job. They'd be able to work things out. Suddenly, thinking about the two of them living together, everything seemed so clear, so right. He'd never believed in love at first sight, that destiny tied you to one person, that true love was when you cared more about someone else than yourself. But now he did, on every account. Strangely, the thought felt liberating—that he was in love.

"Actually," the professor sputtered, "I know Hernán Guerrero by reputation only; we've never met. He's one of the city's more renowned *babalaos*, I understand."

"And García-Mesa?"

"Yes, well, ah…we got to know each other when I was doing research for my dissertation in Cuba back in the late fifties, just before the revolution, a long time ago now."

The lieutenant nodded noncommittally. "But isn't it true, Dr. Krajewski, that you and she had a relationship, a sexual relationship?"

Miguel's eyes got big. You gotta be kidding? he thought. The professor and Rosa?

Krajewski's face flushed and he grinned awkwardly. "Oh, I suppose you could say that, yes."

"And isn't it true that a child, a daughter, was born of that relationship?"

The professor's head and shoulders slumped and he stared at the floor awhile, light reflecting off his nearly bald head. Finally, eyes still downcast, he said, "Rosa was pregnant when I left Cuba, you see. I was out of money and time, and had to get back to Berkeley, to school. I had no choice in the matter, really. My graduate career was at stake. I planned on returning to the island of course, just as soon as I could. But," he shrugged, "within a month I received the letter from Rosa." He glanced over at Gutiérrez, "Saying that our baby girl, Ileana, had died."

"Ileana?" Miguel croaked out loud incredulously.

"That's what she told me she'd named her, Ileana María Luisa."

Gutiérrez said, "Professor, have you recently been given reason to believe that your daughter might still be alive and living in Miami under the name of Ileana Acosta?"

Miguel bolted from his chair. "My girlfriend? That Ileana Acosta?"

"Now, I don't know for sure," the professor said empathically, gesturing with his hands for Miguel to take it easy. "I didn't want to even mention the possibility until I'd spoken with Rosa, but...unfortunately, she won't deny or confirm it."

"That isn't necessary," Gutiérrez said. "I'm afraid she's not your daughter, Professor. I've made a positive identification using INS records, and I also had a friend in the Cuban government check the files in Havana. She was born to Rafael and Catia Acosta several years after your infant child's death, which I also was able to confirm with the priest who officiated at the funeral. Again, I'm sorry."

Miguel breathed a sigh of relief, but then felt a pang of guilt as he watched the professor's face stiffen and his lips become thin and white around the corners. He strained to hear him mumble something about it being too fantastic to believe in the first place.

After a moment, the professor cocked his head and his eyes tightened on Gutiérrez. "If you knew that she wasn't my daughter," he said, his voice rising, cracking slightly, "then I don't understand or appreciate your line of questioning, Lieutenant."

Gutiérrez's expression remained calm, compassionate. "I wasn't being coy or trying to entrap you, Professor. I asked only if recently you'd been given reason to believe that, by some miracle perhaps, she might still be alive." The lieutenant closed his eyes and began to massage them with one hand. "I'm focusing on Ileana, both the deceased child and Ileana Acosta, because I think she, or they, might explain the motivation for a possible murder attempt in two weeks. It might also shed light on the potential victim or victims."

"In what way?" Miguel asked.

Gutiérrez opened his eyes, more weary-looking now than before, and slowly shook his head. "I'm not sure, exactly. That's one of the reasons why I wanted to see both of you this morning. I was hoping you'd be able to fill in some of the gaps that remain in my..." he glanced over at the professor, "thesis concerning the forthcoming murder attempt."

"You mean, that a murder attempt will occur in two weeks, that thesis?" Miguel asked.

"No," Gutiérrez answered. "I have another in mind, which I'll share with you momentarily."

"And it concerns Ileana?" Miguel asked.

Gutiérrez nodded. "Ileana is a link between the two of you, and the three suspects, especially García-Mesa."

"Yes, of course," the professor blurted out, "but that alone seems hardly sufficient to establish a motivation for murder."

"Quite right, Professor. I'll admit the motivation issue troubles me. It just doesn't fit the pattern. But...it might be fear that she has revealed something that could further implicate the suspects in the previous murders. Or it could be just basic human emotions such as..." he looked at Miguel, "jealousy. Or a feeling perhaps..." now his eyes shifted to the professor, "of betrayal."

Krajewski cleared his throat. "Then you've ruled out that the motivation might be purely ritualistic?"

"That's what troubles me, because I can't rule that out entirely. What I'm more confident about is the linkage between Ileana and the potential murder victim or victims."

Miguel said, "Then you have an idea who the victim might be."

"Yes, I do. And that's the second reason why I wanted to see the two of you. Unfortunately, I've come to believe that one of you is the intended victim, even both of you possibly."

The professor reached for a pipe and was soon engulfed in a cloud of smoke he did not bother to fan away for well over a minute. Then he said to Gutiérrez, "Is that the thesis you spoke of earlier?"

"I'm afraid so. However, you can rest assured that we'll provide complete, around-the-clock protection. You'll have nothing to fear. Actually, this is the break we've been looking for. Now, for the first time in these skull murders, we have not only suspects but also potential victims."

It was odd, Miguel thought, but he found that he wasn't even the least bit frightened at this news. Maybe it just hadn't sunk in yet that his life was in danger. Or maybe his confidence in the lieutenant was so deep that, as irrational and perhaps as foolish as it seemed, he simply felt things would be okay. But beyond those considerations, he had in the back of his mind that only when this bizarre situation was finally resolved would he and Ileana have a chance for a new life together.

"Maybe this is naive," he said to Gutiérrez, "but why can't you arrest these people right now if you're convinced they're the ones who committed the murders."

"In truth I might be able to bring charges against them. However, the District Attorney is of the opinion that what we have is insufficient to stand up in court. No eye witnesses, no fingerprints. Just lots of circumstantial evidence. You can hardly get a conviction in a capital murder case with just that."

The professor said, "Still, if they were arrested and held for at least two weeks, then you would have successfully thwarted a potential murder attempt."

"Yes, and in the process possibly squandered an opportunity to bring these killers to justice."

"And how might that be accomplished?" the professor asked.

"I'm afraid they'd have to be caught in the act."

"Of attempted murder, you mean?" Miguel asked.

Gutiérrez nodded. "In order to ensure conviction, yes."

The professor leaned back in his chair, still puffing mightily on the pipe. "I think I see where you're leading. What you're proposing, is it not, is for one of us to serve as a kind of guinea pig?"

"If that's the case," Miguel said, sitting up in his chair and raising his hand as if in a classroom, "then I'd like to volunteer."

"Absolutely not," the professor said with finality. "I won't further endanger the life of this student. If anyone should volunteer, it's me."

Gutiérrez crossed his arms and smiled at them. "Your offers of cooperation are appreciated. And both accepted."

The professor scowled.

"I understand your concern," the lieutenant said to him. "But if we're to be successful, it's critical that over the next two weeks nothing be done to alert them of our intentions. Things have to appear absolutely normal. Should either of you behave out of character, it could tip our hand. Everyone's complete cooperation is essential. Agreed?"

They nodded, and said in unison, "Agreed."

"Then let me explain what I think will happen on the 4th, and what we need to do to prepare for it."

Gutiérrez went on to tell them that he suspected there'd be a party on *Shangó's* feast day...to which they would be invited. He felt it'd probably take place somewhere along the Miami River. But that in all likelihood they wouldn't be informed of the precise location until shortly before party time. It was then they were to contact him to coordinate their final plan of action. Although he hoped they would learn of the location in advance, they weren't to inquire about it. And if by any chance they were going to be picked up and escorted to the party, they were not to worry. They would be followed.

Once Gutiérrez was finished, he thanked them again for their cooperation.

"How did you figure out who the suspects are?" Krajewski heard himself blurting out one last, obviously tactless question.

Gutiérrez smiled wryly. "Actually, Professor, you contributed to the discovery. You see, after I'd exhausted the leads I had, I began making the rounds of all the *botánicas*, hoping I might come up with something...anything. At the Botánica Yemayá, I came across Hernán Guerrero. I'd questioned him years earlier regarding one of the previous murders. Although he had been cleared, I had always had some reservations about him. I remembered the cantaloupe. He was busy with a customer and didn't see me. Not wanting to alarm him, I decided it was best to leave before he became aware of my presence. But, I did see Ileana." Gutiérrez looked warmly over at Miguel. "Congratulations. She's a vision of beauty."

Miguel noticed that the lieutenant's eyes twinkled when he said that. He would have never guessed Gutiérrez capable of such a thing; he appeared so...disillusioned, so saddened by life.

"With nothing more than that to go on," Gutiérrez continued, "I launched a full investigation of Guerrero's background and activities and had him placed under surveillance. Gradually, all the pieces fit together."

Miguel said, "Then it really was a lucky hunch."

"Yes, I suppose so."

Under his breath the professor grumbled, "Let's hope your luck holds."

Among the more pagan of the native practices that substitute for the True Religion is one called *mayombe*, found in the western region where several Bantu-speaking tribes hold sway. Followers of this heathen cult, known as *mayombes*, worship an innumerable host of deities and idols. Yet the focus of their misguided devotion is on the dead, especially the skulls of the deceased, which are considered to be sacred sources of undying power. In their confused theology, these heedless infidels believe that his presumed power can be released by certain rituals and used to invigorate the strength of their so-called gods, thus gaining their favor.

Few of these savage rituals are more evil than the one to *Shangó*, reportedly a Yoruba deity of thunder and lightning who is widely accepted here as Congolese by birth. In this wanton bloodfest, a skull is disinterred from its grave and kept in the open for precisely half a moon or 14 days. At this time it has supposedly reached its maximum power as the pressure of the underworld has been unburdened. The skull is then ceremoniously placed in a large iron kettle called a *prenda*, a vessel for *Shangó's* rejuvenation. Before the power of the skull can be transferred to this deity, however, a human being must be sacrificed and his still-warm blood used to anoint the skull.

According to legend, the demented souls who perform this murderous and sinful act are given leave to dwell at the foot of *Shangó* in his various shrines and forest temples.

Fray Francisco Delgado Arreola, *The Congo: A Basin of Christian Challenge* (The Catholic Mission Press, 1889).

20

POWER OF THE PRENDA

"And so they decided to name me in her memory." Ileana took a sip of coffee and smiled across the restaurant at Miguel and his grandmother. "I'm told Catia, my mother, was very sentimental that way. And of course she loved Rosa so much and felt so bad for her that she'd lost her baby."

She stared reflectively at the demitasse a moment before continuing. "I guess this'll sound crazy since I was too young to really know her, and she's been dead for so many years now. But there are times when I miss my mother so badly I want to cry."

Abuela reached out and took the girl's hand in hers. "It's only natural that you should, Ileana. I still miss my mother and I'm an old woman, as everybody in this place can see."

The three of them chuckled gently and looked around the mirrored walls of the loud and crowded Café Versailles in the heart of Little Havana.

"Maybe that's one of the reasons why," Ileana went on. "I've tried to support Rosa and not criticize the things she's done that I don't agree with."

Miguel said, "You mean, because of your mother's feelings toward her?"

She nodded. "And I know I probably shouldn't feel that way, especially if what my Aunt Salima said is true."

Miguel raised his eyebrows. "What exactly did your aunt say?"

"I once overheard her say to one of her friends that Rosa was insanely jealous of Catia."

He asked why.

"I suppose it had something to do with my father, Rafael."

"I've seen the pictures you have of him," Miguel added. "He was a very handsome man. Do you think Rosa was in love with him too, was that it?"

She shrugged. "According to Aunt Salima, yes, although my mother was completely unaware of it. In fact, my aunt said that had Catia known about it she never would have married my father. That's how much she loved Rosa."

Abuela said, "I've known of women who care more about the happiness of others than their own. They're very special people. You should feel proud of her, Ileana."

Abuela drank the last of her coffee and made a sour face. "Sadly, I've known women like Rosa, too. You'll have to be very careful these next two weeks, especially on the 4th, of course." She clasped her hands together as if in prayer. "The Virgin knows how I'll worry every minute. I will pray constantly. But you are doing the right thing by helping the *policía*. Just don't do anything foolish, and remember to follow the lieutenant's advice. Don't let them think you know something is wrong."

She smiled at Miguel. "And I suppose that means you'll have to keep going to her house every night."

He and Ileana grinned at each other and leaned together, touching shoulders.

"Okay, here they come," Miguel announced, glancing up at the approaching waiter. "You'll see, they serve the best *medianoches* in all the world."

The grandmother rolled her eyes.

"Except for Cuba, of course," he added quickly.

When they had finished the sandwiches and were waiting for their dessert of *fruta bomba* (papaya) milk shakes, Abuela said to Miguel, "You once asked me if'd I'd ever heard of a skull being stolen from a grave. At the time I said no, but I've since recalled such an occasion. It was one summer when I was a young girl and we were vacationing in the mountains, as we often did to escape the heat of Havana. One night there, in a little negro village not far from where we were staying, a *cráneo*, a skull, was taken from the cemetery. I remember Sara, our maid, going over there to talk with the villagers about it and becoming very nervous and upset."

"Was someone murdered two weeks later?" Miguel asked hurriedly.

"I don't remember how long it was, but yes, there was a horrible murder: A woman's head was chopped off with a sword and replaced by that stolen skull. That's how they found her, sitting in the corner with that skull stuck right where her head used to be. Sara learned that the old *santero* who'd done it had lost his mind and kept telling everybody that they soon would return to Africa if they obeyed the ancient ways. Then, only several days later, the authorities located him and took him away. He was never heard from again. Of course, I was very frightened by all this. My family wouldn't speak of it around me."

"That's too bad," Miguel muttered, shaking his head. "If we knew why he, the old *santero*, had done it, we might understand something about the murders here."

"Well," Abuela drawled, a half-smile on her wrinkled face, "Sara did tell me a thing or two about it. She said the villagers had told her that the blood was used by the old man to feed the *prenda*."

"The iron cauldron?" Miguel asked.

"Yes, that's right. It was said that offerings of human blood would increase its power and greatly please the *orisha* who owns the *prenda*: *Shangó*."

They stared at each other silently, until Miguel furrowed his brow and said, "But that just doesn't fit with anything I've ever heard or read about the cult. I was under the impression that *santería* didn't deal in revenge or sanction human death.

Those are supposed to be forms of black magic, and it practices only white magic."

Abuela said, "I don't know about this black and white magic business. But I agree that it's unusual, unlike anything I've ever seen in *regla de ocha*, what you call *santería*. That's what interested Sara, too. But she told me those villagers there were different. They didn't speak any Yoruba and their ancestors had come from…the Congo, I think she said."

"Then they probably were Bantu people," Miguel added. "Still, that doesn't explain why a skull had to be stolen two weeks before the *prenda* could be fed."

Abuela gestured emphatically with both hands. "I know, I know it doesn't. But I've told you everything that Sara told me. Maybe you've got more reading to do, Miguel."

The old lady looked up and smiled broadly at the waiter. "Well, look at these!"

She was right, Miguel realized. He did have more reading to do. The next day he sought out Professor Krajewski for references to books and articles on Bantu religions, thinking it would be the logical place to start. The professor had been helpful as usual, but expressed little apparent interest in the story his grandmother had related, and appeared extremely nervous and preoccupied; more than once he'd asked if he had heard anything about the party for *Shangó*.

Of course, Miguel could empathize with the professor's feelings. He too felt a mounting sense of strain as he attempted, quite self-consciously he decided, to maintain an appearance of normalcy when his life, possibly, was on the line.

Yet by Saturday, the end of the first week, he had not altered his daily routine except for the extended hours spent in the library, which in itself wasn't unusual. Final examinations were approaching. Unfortunately, despite having gone through nearly 300 books and articles dealing with Bantu religion and culture, he hadn't found a single reference to rituals involving the *prenda*. He was disappointed, but resigned. He would have to continue the search, if for no other reason than the distraction it offered in the daytime when he couldn't be with Ileana.

That evening, lying in bed together at her place, Miguel asked her how it had gone at the *botánica*, whether Hernán had been his usual self.

"Actually," she answered, "he seems even happier than normal, and I think it's because he's expecting Dago to arrive any day now. That's what I heard him say on the phone this morning."

"Then the lieutenant must be right. The three of them work as a team. And the fact that this Dago is on his way down means that he's probably right about there being a murder attempt one week from tonight. Maybe we ought to call the lieutenant and tell him the news."

"Yes, I think that'd be a good idea. Too bad I don't have a phone."

"Yeah, I wish you did too, but for other reasons."

She smiled at him reassuringly.

"I'll call him in the morning," Miguel said, taking her hand and kissing it tenderly if absentmindedly. Shortly he said, "I wonder what role Dago plays in these...murders. It must be important if they have him come down all the way from New Jersey. You've met him, what do you think?"

She frowned. "I only know that Hernán really likes him, thinks that no *santero* can handle *Ogun's* knife as well as he can."

"Then he's probably responsible for the sacrifices, right?"

"Yes, I think that's his speciality, specially of four-legged animals. I don't care for him, the way he looks at me. But I still can't see him, or any of them, killing somebody. Except maybe..."

"Except maybe Rosa?" he finished.

Ileana's eyes dropped and she began toying with her yellow and green bead necklace. "She came in today, Miguel, the first time this week."

"Were you nervous?"

"Only when I first saw her."

"Did she seem, you know, different?"

"No, not really. Rosa's always happy when she's buying offerings and gifts for her *orishas*. She spends thousands on them. Believe me, she's our best customer, and I know she shops at other *botánicas*, too."

He looked puzzled. "Thousands?"

"Oh, yes, easily."

"But where does she get that kind of money? I mean, she couldn't possibly earn that much just doing consultations. Does she have another job?"

Ileana laughed. "She once told me that taking care of her masters was work enough. And I believe her, too, the way she dotes on them. But I don't know where she gets the money. I do know that the angriest I've ever seen her was that time when we were in another *botánica* and she didn't have the money to buy this present she wanted to give *Shangó*. Oh, she was so mad it frightened me. Luckily, I had enough cash on me that I could buy the gift for her, a pair of jade elephants."

"Jade's expensive."

"I know. The elephants cost nearly $3,000."

"You carry that much cash on you?" Miguel asked.

She grinned at him, but evaded the question. "When we were leaving the *botánica* I heard her say something like, 'This should take care of my rent for a while.' I thought that was a strange thing to say because I know she owns her home."

Miguel lay there silently for a few moments, arms crossed behind his head. Finally, a bemused smile on his face, he asked if Rosa had ever shown her the little black rag doll she kept in her *Ile* next to the statue of *Shangó*.

"I've seen it, yes, but she never said anything about it to me. What about you?"

He told her what Rosa had said, that she'd been given permission to live in the *Ile* and that the doll was actually her. He said, "Do you think that she somehow feels indebted to the *orishas* for allowing her to stay here, and that's why she made that comment about paying rent?"

Ileana looked confused and said she'd never heard of such a thing. "But with Rosa, you never know. Maybe she does believe that doll is her."

"Even if that's the case," he said, "what I'd like to know is what she had to do to gain the *orishas'* permission to live there in the first place."

"Oh, Miguel," Ileana said, grabbing his arm, "I forgot to tell you that Rosa left an envelope for you when she was at the *botánica* today. I think I know what it is, but here, I'll get it for you."

Wearing only *Ochún's* necklace, Ileana bounded over to the dresser. Seeing her naked at a distance like this had always excited him—her shoulders thrown back, her beautiful heavy upturned breasts swaying, the motions of her long-legged lithe body smooth as a stream of *latina* femininity. They'd not made love this week, although they'd spent nearly all their time together in bed. Just being that close, feeling the warmth, the comfort, the security, had been enough.

"Wanna make love before I open this?" Miguel asked, holding up the envelope she'd just handed him.

Without saying a word, Ileana casually lifted her leg over his chest and straddled him.

Miguel pulls out Lieutenant Gutiérrez's card. He has instructions to call any time, day or night. His home phone number is handwritten across the top. It is 9:15, Sunday morning. He tries the Department number first.

Gutiérrez answers.

He already knows that Dago will be arriving in Miami shortly, a fact which gives Miguel great relief. It tells him that the lieutenant is on top of the situation. He tells Gutiérrez that Rosa has sent a card by way of Ileana. Miguel, the professor and the girl are to attend "A Celebration in Honor of the Feast Day of the *Orisha, Shangó*." As the lieutenant has predicted, the party is scheduled for next Saturday night, beginning at 11 o'clock.

"I assume she didn't give you an address," Gutiérrez says lightly.

"No, just that she'll call me about it later."

The lieutenant sounds as calm as a sleeping cat. It's good news, he says. "Knowing the location in advance, even if only a few hours before things get under way, will work in our favor. Remember, you're to call me as soon as she gets in touch with you, and I'll take it from there. Both she and Guerrero are under surveillance, so there's a chance we could learn of the location before she calls."

· "Oh, does she have an RSVP on the invitation?" Gutiérrez asks.

Miguel hesitates. Then soft laughter on the other end of the line tells him the lieutenant is joking.

"So, I gather you and and Ileana are holding up okay."

"Yeah, we're doing okay, especially Ileana. But if I were in her position, we'd have something to worry about. I'm not sure I could handle the pressure."

"You might surprise yourself with what you can do under pressure, Miguel. But, yes, I agree Ileana's been very brave. Professor Krajewski has to relax a bit, though. He's called every day this week. But he'll come through, too. You wait and see."

It's Friday. Miguel has found what he is looking for only minutes before the library closes. He was headed out of the African stacks when he spots the thick, red, hard-covered tome by Francisco Delgado Arreola, a 19th century Jesuit missionary-geographer. He had made a photocopy of the critical passage from the book and dashed through the large glass door of the library just as the lights were flickering off.

Now it's nearly midnight. Miguel and his grandmother are sitting in the living room watching the first Presto log of the winter season burn quietly and evenly in the fireplace. His mind is a battlefield of mixed emotions, alternately anxious and confident, confused and resolved. Physically, he feels as in his high school days before a football game—dry-mouthed, tight in the stomach, and curiously fighting a bout of sleepiness though he is not the slightest bit tired.

He has yet to hear from Rosa, and has therefore postponed calling the lieutenant. Earlier, however, he has phoned Professor Krajewski with the news of his discovery. "A startling find," Krajewski labels it. Surprisingly, considering Gutiérrez's comments to the contrary, the professor sounds remarkably relaxed and affable over the phone. What gives him away is the request that Miguel and Ileana pick him up the following evening. "It's getting where I don't much care to drive at night anymore," the professor says.

Obviously, Dr. Krajewski does not want to face the ordeal alone. But there is strength in numbers, Miguel decides. "Sure, we'd be glad to pick you up," he replies.

Abuela breaks the silence. "It looks like she won't call until tomorrow."

Miguels shrugs. "I still think she'll call tonight. But maybe you're right."

"Can I get you something, another *café* maybe?"

Miguel smiles at her warmly, but shakes his head no.

"You're worried about the girl, aren't you?"

"I don't like leaving her alone, not tonight especially."

"I know that, Miguelito. But she's stronger than you probably think. Did I tell you that she's called me from the *botánica* every day this week?"

Miguel is startled into attention.

"It's okay, don't worry. She called only when the *babalao* wasn't there."

"What'd you talk about?"

"Oh, her life, a little of everything, this and that. Imagine a shy young girl, an only child from a prominent and wealthy family being exposed to the black *santos* at an early age, living an isolated, sheltered life. Now...imagine that I am this young girl. That's right, Ileana and I have much in common. Of course, I was already married at her age and was carrying your mother."

Miguel pauses. "So, what do you do think of her?"

"She has much to recommend her." Abuela waits a moment. She grins, then she announces, "Yes, I recommend her."

They scoot over on the couch closer to one another and hug.

Miguel holds his grandmother's hands, his eyes downcast slightly, his voice suddenly hesitant. "There's...only one thing that bothers me about her, about us. I just remember you saying that if she wore that necklace, the *collares* of *Ochún*, that she'd be a daughter of the *orisha* for life. I'm not sure if I'm prepared for that."

The old woman squeezes her grandson's hands. "The commitment is only what you make it, Miguel. I've spoken to her about it. She feels as I do: The faith isn't bad, but there are some bad people in it, just as there are in all religions. Like me, she's more a Catholic than a follower of *santería*."

Miguel says, "What do you mean, like you?"

Abuela releases his hands, reaches inside her dress and pulls out a yellow and green bead necklace. *El collar de Ochún.*

The phone rings.

"I didn't think you'd be at Ileana's tonight," Rosa informs Miguel.

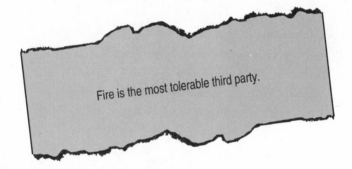

Fire is the most tolerable third party.

Henry David Thoreau, *Journal*

21

OH, WHAT A PARTY!

The professor was waiting at the head of the driveway in front of his sprawling house on Riviera Drive in the Gables. He squinted into the glare of the approaching headlights, then looked around disorientedly, not quite sure of what he was doing out there beyond the fortress of his house. But the car pulled up and he saw it was Miguel rolling down the window. He grinned, relieved, and gave a quick little conspiratorial wave.

"Professor Krajewski, I'd like you to meet Ileana Acosta, my fiancée. Ileana. Professor Krajewski."

She extended her hand. "I've heard so much about you, Professor."

"And I have also heard about you," he responded warmly, taking her hand. "May I say...you're even more beautiful than I had imagined."

She blinked her eyes once very slowly.

"I hadn't realized," he said, "that you two were engaged."

"Oh, yes," Miguel deadpanned, "for at least an hour now."

They laughed.

"Well," the professor said, "I suppose we ought to get this over with so we can come back and celebrate your engagement properly. I know of a wonderful restaurant for such an occasion, and we'll invite your grandmother, too, Miguel. The treat's mine, of course."

"Now," he sighed, turning to look with apparent concern at the car, "is there going to be enough room for all of us in this...hot rod."

"There is," Miguel replied, a thin smile on his face, "if you wouldn't mind Ileana sitting on your lap. We're not going that far."

"Of course not," the professor drawled, then gangly crawled in the Z, barely able to suppress his glee.

There was an irrepressible gaiety that filled the car as it sped south down Dixie Highway, past the University, South Miami, Kendall and on toward the address in Perrine that Rosa had given Miguel the night before. Along the way, they laughed at everything they said or saw, no matter how mundane—the people on the streets, the Metrorail stations, Shorty's Barbeque place, Connie Banko's Bikini shop.

The giddiness was a cover, of course. All three recognized that. It reminded Miguel of his Uncle Infante's funeral when everyone in the family, seated together in separate pews at the side of the parlor, kept laughing and carrying on as they watched the mourners, their friends and distant relatives, file past the open coffin. Finally, Aunt Julia had begun to whimper, and within seconds the family was in tears.

Just as suddenly, the mood in the car changed.

Ileana reported in a soft voice. "Last night, after midnight, I caught Dago peeking in my window. I think he was getting ready to break in. Quick as I could, I jumped to the window, to make sure it was locked. Then I heard Rosa's voice yell at Dago from Hernán's. It was really weird what she said. She yelled at Dago, 'I warned you to stay away from that bitch; that bitch is just like her mother.' I'm sure that's what I heard her say."

"What did he do then?" Miguel asked.

"Dago left finally, cussing and flipping his middle finger up at the window where she stood watching him."

The professor patted the girl reassuringly on the back. "She's demented, Ileana, quite demented indeed. A brilliant woman. But not the most stable. Even back in Cuba, she couldn't handle the pressure of writing her thesis. Out of desperation, she asked me to finish it for her. I did it willingly, of course."

Miguel glanced over at the professor.

"I know what you're thinking, Miguel, but remember. The foolishness of a man in love knows no bounds. And believe me, I was in love with her, deeply so. Of course I wasn't much of a catch at the time. But she was fond of me...in her own way, I suppose."

The professor cleared his throat, changing the subject. He wanted to know what Gutiérrez had told Miguel the night before.

"They'll have a full squad ready to surround the place at a moment's notice. They might even bug the house...plant an officer or two from the SWAT team inside the place maybe... in a closet...the attic. But we have to stay calm, regardless of what happens, he insisted. We have to trust him," Miguel enumerated.

As he spoke, Miguel made a turn. The Z cut off Coral Reef Drive onto S.W. 72nd Avenue, proceeding to the address at 16731, less than a mile away. A dark, rolling stretch of road, S.W. 72nd was lined with a forest of pines and oaks pushing out from a thick undergrowth of ferns and palmetto bushes. A heavy fog hangs over the top of the trees, blocking out the faint light of the moon.

Miguel feels that something is wrong, terribly wrong. But he cannot avoid whatever awaits them down a dip in the road. He sees Rosa at the bottom. She stands behind her Buick Skylark, parked sideways, blocking both traffic lanes. Miguel slams on the brakes, turns the wheel sharply. The Z skids wildly. It halts just short of the Buick. Rosa, dressed in a heavy blood-red robe with white trim, opens the door on the driver's side of the Z. Her head is now poked in the car, only inches from Miguel's face, staring with amused, liquid eyes and flaring nostrils at Ileana and the professor.

"Well, isn't this cozy," she hisses, her voice like a viper.

Miguel jerks his face away to avoid Rosa's breath, searing hot and reeking of smoldering soot, as if the gates of hell itself had suddenly flung open.

"As you might have guessed, there's been a slight change of plans. Oh, don't look so surprised now. We can't be too cautious, can we?"

Rosa laughs demonically. Miguel feels like throwing up, the scalding, putrid smell is so overwhelming.

"You can park over there," she orders, pointing to a small clearing on the right side of the road. "We'll take my car. There's much more room. But Henry, you do look so very happy with that little cunt on your lap. And I bet she loves it, too. Now don't you, bitch?"

Rosa's hand slips around Miguel's upper arm. He glances tentatively up at her. She squeezes hard, effortlessly it seems to him, smiling sardonically all the while. Miguel's arm instantly goes numb, crushed in the vice grip of Rosa's extraordinarily powerful hand. Rosa who is...*Shangó*, that is.

"Now pull over there," Rosa commands, releasing her grip with a fetching grin. "We don't want to be late for my party."

Miguel climbs in the front seat of the Buick, looks back at Ileana, at the professor. His lips move with the message to...stay calm.

They wind and twist through the streets of Perrine. The seediness of the town, with its depressed neighborhoods and battered buildings, envelopes their silence for ten minutes or more. But the car reverberates, literally pulsates, with the ponderous sounds of Rosa's labored breathing. A stench—a heavy stench born of sacrificed animals, of rotting fruit and burnt offerings, Miguel decides—has diffused throughout the car. The trapped air becomes fetid. Finally, Rosa pulls up in front of an old, isolated Victorian farmhouse on the western edge of Perrine's city limits.

Miguel pushes open the door and breathes deeply the fresh air. Ileana and the professor cough and gulp in air also as they clamber out of the car onto the darkened street.

Rosa laughs to herself obnoxiously. She leads them down a long driveway to a detached wooden garage behind the crumbling Victorian house.

The garage is shut, but as they get closer a beam of light streams along the bottom of the door. The faint sounds of voices coming from inside can be heard.

Rosa pulls open the sliding door. She stands by the threshold, waiting for the three of them to enter. Miguel notices a heavy brass lock hanging from a new hinge and latch on the door. He swallows hard to suppress a sudden feeling of panic racing through his body and clogging his throat.

A makeshift altar stands in the center of the garage. A human skull rests prominently inside a large iron cauldron surrounded by burning incense and candles. Propitiatory gifts—platters of fruits, nuts and candies, and bottles of liquor are spread before the altar. A large angel food cake rests at its base. Written across it in red icing is, *"Felicidades Shangó!"* Off in a corner of the room are several chickens in cages and a cowering goat, tied with a thick, twisted rope.

Hernán and Dago, who'd been sitting on bundles of old newspaper stacked against the back wall, stand staring in bewilderment at the four new arrivals.

"Where's the guy you tole us about, tha' guy who want to become an *hermano* of the *santos?*" Dago asks Rosa.

Not giving her a chance to answer, Hernán butts in, "Ileana, what are *you* doing here. And you, Miguel? And who is this man?"

"Yes, well," Rosa said smartly. She claps her hands twice and says, "He'll be along shortly." Then, looking at Miguel,

Ileana and Krajewski, she adds, "And these people, why...they're our honored guests. They've come to help celebrate my feast day.

"Dr. Henry Krajewski, an expert on our religion," she announces, pointing formally to the professor, and then snorts out loud a couple of times in an alternately bemused and disgusted manner.

"Miguel Calderón, one of the distinguished professor's students and spies, a young man who has already been caught sabotaging one of our most sacred rituals."

Rosa pauses as her voice becomes heavy with anger. "And the little bitch herself, his lover and fellow conspirator."

Dago was grinning from ear to ear at all of this, but Hernán seemed both confused and hurt.

"Why are you talking about the girl like this?" he questioned.

"Never mind," Rosa barked. "Let the party begin at once. We've wasted enough time already."

Hernán and Dago look at each other and laugh. "At once?" Dago mocks. "Maybe you forget who we are, woman. What's this, 'Let-the-party-begin-at-once crap?'"

You heard me, little man!" Rosa thunders. "I said at once. Yes, I *command* you to begin the party this very instant!"

"And who are you to command us?" Hernán questions. "Have you forgotten that I am the *babalao* here?"

"*Babalao*," Rosa huffs derisively, then spits on the floor. "*Babalaos* and *santeros* are nothing in the presence of *Shangó*! Now, I'll say it once again: Let the party begin."

For the first time, Dago stopped grinning.

Hernán said, "*Shangó* hasn't been called down. There's been no music, no offerings, no respect. You haven't made the saint; it isn't possible. I've heard enough of you. Now move out of the way, woman, we're leaving." He started toward the door, then looked over at Ileana and in an impatient voice said, "Come on with me...the three of you!"

"Oh?" Rosa drawled, putting her hands on her hips. "I think you'd better stay. This is a very special occasion. You don't want to miss it. In fact, it wouldn't be the same without you." Laughter erupted from her mouth, smirking, hideous, deafening. Suddenly, the temperature in the room rose by no less than twenty degrees. The smell of hot, burning coals—or was it something else, something more organic?—was undeniable.

At the door, Hernán attempted to push by, swatting at her like a bothersome fly. Rosa stopped laughing. In a split second she grabbed his massive arm, then yanked the huge man like a hapless doll across the room where he smashed amid a flurry of feathers into the chicken cages against the far wall.

Stealthily, while all eyes were glued on Hernán and the squawking chickens, Dago sneaked along the side wall toward the door. Rosa spotted him. In a flash she reached out and grabbed him by the shoulder and spun him around. He came out of the spin with a slight grin on his face and *Ogun's* knife in his hand. He lunged toward Rosa's belly. But as smoothly and skillfully as the most accomplished matador, she stepped aside at the last perilous second.

Dago splatted on his stomach, the knife still in his hand. Like a water bug, he instantly flipped over onto his back, struggling to get up. Rosa bounded over and with one heavy, powerful stomp of her foot smashed Dago's head, crushing it.

Miguel, frozen in place not ten feet away, watched in horror as Dago's eyes popped out and two streams of blood gushed from his nostrils.

The knife fell from the dwarf's limp hand.

Ileana screamed and clutched for Miguel as the professor turned and gagged.

From the back of the garage, Hernán, on hands and knees, bellowed at the smirking Rosa. "You're not *Shangó*! An *orisha* would never do this...this evil."

Now on his feet and beside himself with rage, Hernán lowered his head and like a wounded bull wildly charged Rosa's blood-red robe.

Immediately Rosa prepared to meet him, dropping into a linebacker's stance—knees bent, butt down, back straight, head cocked.

The impact of their collision was bone-jarring as Rosa delivered a tremendous forearm shiver to Hernán's upper chest and neck. The powerful blow caused the giant's head to snap back, arching his body in half. He slumped to the floor, eyes rolling.

As Rosa gathered herself, Miguel realized this was the moment to take action, to do something. His body moved toward the knife on the floor next to Dago. In a scoop he grabs it.

"Go!" he yells to Ileana and the professor. "Get out of here!"

The girl hesitates, but then, reading the look on Miguel's face, dashes for the door.

But this action is not lost on Rosa. "Oh no, you little cunt. You're not going anywhere. Except to hell."

Rosa scrambles toward the door to block the exist. Miguel charges at her, wielding the knife above his head. With all his strength he plunges the eight-inch blade down, aiming directly for her face.

Confidently, easily, Rosa grabs his wrist with one hand; with the other she catches Ileana by her hair as the girl attempts to sprint by.

Seizing the opportunity, Miguel slams his left fist into the side of Rosa's head, hitting her solidly on the ear. She grimaces, her face now distorted into the unmistakable form of a black male. Then she reverts back to normal. Miguel can't believe what he has seen.

With a powerful motion Rosa whips both he and Ileana to the floor. The girl screams out in pain, and Miguel feels his wrist crushed.

The knife falls free.

Rosa bends over to pick it up. And when she does, the professor rams her from behind, his head hitting her squarely on the buttocks, sending her sprawling half way out the door.

Rosa gets up on her knees, looks back at the professor, and smiles with amusement. "You're such a fool, Henry. Always putting your head into places it doesn't belong."

In a second she sprang to her feet. "Well," she howls, "I guess you people just aren't in the mood for a party."

And with that she steps outside and slams the door shut behind her.

Miguel heard the lock click.

On the far side of the garage, Rosa picked up a red five-gallon gas can and a box of wooden matches. She walked back to the front of the structure near the door, unscrewed the cap and began to splash gasoline against the garage.

Those fools. Those ungrateful, selfish fools. How dare they refuse to honor my day! How dare they dishonor *Shangó*! That *santero*...the way he used *Ogun's* knife...thought he was an *orisha*. An *orisha*! And that fat bastard child of *Yemayá*, the old sea hag herself, calls himself a *babalao*. Haw! He knows nothing of the future. He's an imposter! He deserves what's coming. They all deserve what's coming! That includes you, too, learned professor, expert on *santería*. Oh, yes, it most certainly includes you! You who abandoned my faithful, loving servant Rosa...Rosa...Rosa. But, oh, Henrito, poor silly Henrito, you could have stayed, it would've worked out, then our child—our child!—would have... No! No! Can you deny that you've earned *Shangó's* punishment? Or your spy student? Or his girlfriend? Why, when I think back on all that Rosa has done for...

"Happy feast day, *Shangó!* Happy feast day!"

Rosa spun around, spilling gas on her robe as she did.

Lieutenant Gutiérrez was crouched over in shooting position, both arms extended, the Smith & Wesson pointing directly at the can.

Rosa let her shoulders slump and she smiled wanly at the lieutenant. "Put that away," she whined. "You can't shoot an unarmed woman, a poor old middle-aged defenseless lady, now can you?"

There was no expression on Gutiérrez's face when the .38 slug hit the can, sending a fireball soaring into the darkened evening sky.

For a moment he coldly watched Rosa whirl about the driveway, totally engulfed in flames. Then he stepped over to the garage and casually shot the lock off the door. Cautiously, Gutiérrez pulled it open.

Miguel, Ileana and the professor were huddled together, their eyes bulging.

"Thank God," the professor sighed. "I was afraid we were history."

Gutiérrez surveyed the scene. On the floor Hernán was beginning to stir. Dago lay awkwardly, lifelessly on his back, his face caked in blood.

"So you're okay?" the lieutenant said.

Before anyone could answer, Ileana gasped and covered her mouth, her eyes fixed on Rosa.

Not twenty feet away, Rosa had stopped dead in her tracks and had begun to laugh hysterically.

A bored look on his face, Gutiérrez turned toward Rosa and with the same casualness in which he'd shot off the lock on the door, pumped four slugs into her flaming body.

Rosa laughed no more.

Joe's Key Lime Pie Recipe

Ingredients:

One 14-ounce can sweetened condensed milk
Four egg yolks
Four ounces key lime juice

Combine milk and egg yolks at low speed. Slowly add juice, mixing until well blended. Pour into nine-inch graham cracker pie shell. Refrigerate overnight. Bake at 350° for eight minutes. Top with whipped cream.

22
STONE CRABS AND KEY LIME PIE

Gutiérrez closed the folder on his desk and leaned back in his swivel chair. He smiled admiringly over at the professor, Ileana, Miguel and his grandmother. "Now don't you all look magnificent tonight, just magnificent."

He nodded appreciatively at the four of them, decked out in suits and evening dresses, clustered together at the door of his office, smiling at him broadly. "I do wish I could join you. It's just that," he glanced with pained resignation around the cramped, sterile room, "I've got some paperwork I shouldn't postpone any longer."

"Come now, Lieutenant," the professor insisted. "Paperwork can always wait. We're dining at Joe's Stone Crab. My treat mind you, and no sane man should ever turn down a free meal at Joe's."

"I see your point," Gutiérrez laughed. "But anyone foolish enough to be a cop for as long as I, has a right to act a little insane from time to time."

"Well," the professor said snappishly, "if you won't reconsider, rest assured we'll raise a toast in your honor. Shall we?" he asked the ladies, extending his open hand toward the door.

"*Un momento*," Abuela sighed in a tired voice, stepping over to the lieutenant's cluttered desk. "Now, you can't expect me to eat and drink and enjoy myself when my mind's full of questions only you can answer."

He smiled at her understandingly. "I know it's probably not enough to just accept that matters worked out. Of course, *señora*, I'll be glad to answer your questions. I had planned on clearing the air anyway, at some point."

She raised her eyebrows and shrugged her shoulders and said to him directly, "Okay then: How did you find them?"

"Yes," the professor added, "please fill us in on *that* one, if you would."

Gutiérrez leaned back further in the chair and clasped his hands behind his head. "Fortunately, I had kept a detailed log of where García-Mesa had been the preceding week, based on our surveillance of her activities. She had stopped by that garage only once, several days before...*Shangó's* party. And even then, she didn't stay all that long. What really threw me though was the amount of time and effort she spent on preparing the house on S.W. 72nd. Even that afternoon, she was in there for hours, setting up the altar, bringing in food and drinks and the animals. It was really quite an elaborate hoax."

Miguel said, "Then she must have known that she was being followed."

"I suspect she did, but perhaps she was just being cautious. At any rate, she managed to lose our tail late that evening, just before the party. And to complicate matters, we couldn't locate the other two throughout the day. Still, I was confident the gathering would be at the house on 72nd. But when you didn't show up, I went through the log and," he grinned at them shyly, "took a hunch where you'd be."

Abuela crossed herself.

"I have to ask then," the professor said, "why you didn't have our car followed."

Gutiérrez sat up in the chair and tapped his fingers on the desk. "To put it simply, Professor, my request was turned down. It was all a matter of petty economics. And that's one of the reasons why I turned in my badge this morning. I've had enough."

Everyone looked around at each other silently for a moment. Then the professor said, "Well the police department has certainly lost a good man. Will you retire to the Dominican Republic as planned?"

"Yes, just as soon as the inquiry is over."

"Inquiry?" the professor questioned.

"They're investigating García-Mesa's death. There was some concern about excessive use of deadly force."

The professor sputtered, "But surely they couldn't question your actions; they were entirely appropriate in my judgment, and I'll be more than happy to tell them as much."

Gutiérrez winked at him. "That won't be necessary. There are some advantages to being an old cop. It's all a formality, really. The Chief and I have already discussed the situation."

"What I don't understand," Miguel said to the lieutenant, "is why Rosa needed Hernán and Dago. I mean, you told us earlier, the day after the party I think it was, that you didn't believe that they were directly involved in the murders. So..." he trailed off.

"That's right," Gutiérrez said. "Hernán swears that he and Dago knew nothing of the murders. And I think he's telling the truth. As to why she needed them... At least until the very end she probably saw nothing wrong in what she was doing—she was just feeding the *prenda*, following ancient rituals, trying to gain the favor of *Shangó*."

"That one was crazy!" Abuela huffed.

"Yes, quite," the professor agreed.

"What'll happen to Hernán?" Ileana asked.

"He's still in Jackson Memorial, recovering from the broken shoulder and a collapsed lung. But he'll eventually be charged with a number of misdemeanors, that's all. Did you know that he paid for Dago's funeral? I understand they had quite a celebration at his wake out in Hialeah. In fact, we even got a complaint from the neighbors that they were making too much noise, singing and dancing all night long. It was the first time we've ever had a complaint for too much noise at a funeral home."

They all laughed.

"Well," Gutiérrez said, smiling at Miguel and Ileana, "what are your plans?

Miguel put his arm around the girl. "We're getting married at the end of the month, on New Year's Eve."

"Then you ought to consider honeymooning in Santo Domingo. You can stay with me. I've got more than enough room."

Abuela laughed out loud and said to the lieutenant, "Now, would you want to spend your honeymoon with an old retired policeman?"

Gutiérrez flushed.

"Thanks for the offer, though," Miguel said. "But we couldn't afford it. I barely have enough saved to get us in a nice apartment. And then I'll have to find a part-time job and just take classes on a part-time basis."

Ileana and Abuela began to giggle.

"What's so funny?" Miguel asked.

Ileana, still giggling, opened her purse and took out a savings deposit passbook and handed it to Miguel.

"We can go on a honeymoon if you like," she said. "And you can still go to school full-time. And we can buy a house too, if you like."

Miguel opened the passbook and saw the balance: $872,341.58.

"What!" he screamed.

"My aunt never trusted Castro," Ileana laughed. "And so she kept most of our money in this country. I think there are three or four other accounts."

"You think?" he cried out.

Laughter filled the room.

Gutiérrez stood up. "You're right, Professor," he said happily, "paperwork can always wait. I'd love to join you. Stone crabs and key lime pie sound wonderful about now."

"Three or four others?" Miguel muttered to no one in particular as they walked out the door.